FOREWORD

If you are reading this, "thank you." I'm going to assume you bought my book.

This is my first time writing prose. In the past I've told stories through comics but something shifted and I now have more of an urge to tell a story than draw the cool scenes.

This book is the result of the old adage 'if you can't find what you want, go make it yourself.' I love power fantasies, overpowered protagonists are fun to me. Unfortunately for me, I have to read through 3 books before the hero becomes the badass I wanted in book one.

There is also the problem of 'Power creep'. If you are familiar with Dragon Ball you get the idea of stronger and stronger enemies who conveniently show up in order to give your hero the next plateau to reach. Eventually your hero is destroying galaxies with a sneeze. There is nowhere to go from there. I'm hoping by giving characters their full power upfront I can force myself to be more creative with how the abilities are used rather than just giving them... more. That being said, I am not above creating my own version of super saiyan. (I can only pray that whatever I end up doing gets to be that popular.)

Enough of my rambling. I hope you enjoy reading the story as much as I enjoyed writing it.

CONTENTS

CHAPTER 1

The Mage Assembly worked their spells trying to determine where they should focus their resources in the coming year. Divination was seldom accurate but with enough broad strokes a useful picture could be formed. The result of their casting was nothing but the spell didn't fail. The spell worked better than most, it not only told them there was nothing it also told them the nothing was coming from the north.

To the North, Tuck stepped out of the cave that hid the lost Temple. It was a bright and beautiful day, the mountain air was crisp with a frosty bite from the freshly fallen snow, he was on a peak overlooking a snow covered forest. In the distance he could see mountain ranges and floating pieces of land. Giant creatures flew through the sky. The world looked untamed… almost. To the South between two peaks Tuck noticed an unnatural structure, the straight lines caught his eye, it must be a settlement. It was weeks away by foot but manageable.

Tuck focused on the settlement, right now his vision was the best it had ever been, so he noticed the relatively smaller things flying about…

"Are those blimps?" He began to wonder when he was seized by instinct.

'MOVE!' it screamed at him.

Before he could physically react. Tuck found himself 3 feet to his left. In the space he just occupied a gigantic white cloaked man crashed into the earth with so much force, the impact shattered the stone and caused a blastwave that threw Tuck even further away.

'That madman would have landed on me if I had not flickered away.' Tuck thought. The odd word 'flicker' was a good description of his supernatural movement just now but he didn't have time to analyse it he studied his attacker. The man's head swivelled around and Tuck found himself looking at a massive cyclopedian eye embedded in the face of an owl.

'A Titan MonoOwl.' Part of his mind recognised. Not even 5 minutes in this world and Tuck already met his first Titan Beast.

The MonoOwl let out a screech and the entire forest seemed to come to life as a flock of its smaller brethren took to flight. It too opened its massive wings and with one mighty beat was airborne.

A small rational part of his mind wondered how something so big could still fly, especially with such speed but the rest of his brain told him to be somewhere else.

Tuck ran, jumped and fell down the hillside. His new endurance, strength and speed surprised him but compared to the flying beast it wasn't enough. Smaller MonoOwls harassed Tuck while their Titan leader tried to finish him. Time and again Tuck's new abilities kept him alive as new instincts kicked in but with an entire forest to clear he wasn't going to make it. Tuck dodged another dive from the Titan MonoOwl but it hit him with a gust of air that blasted him off his feet and slammed him into a thick tree. He was dazed.

'I should have never left the temple.' He thought and just like that, Tuck was jumping through space and popping back out in the Temple where he started. Cut, bleeding, exhausted and probably with a concussion but also wiser and most importantly alive.

Tuck sat down to catch his breath. He looked around the temple, it was spartan. An altar held up by four faceless women was the only furniture. There was no dust on the floor, no spider webs in the high ceiling and although the door was the only opening a beam of light magically illuminated the altar. Tuck instinctively knew the Titan MonoOwl wouldn't enter here. No beast would, the only reason he could enter was that he was an invited guest.

Tuck assessed himself, his shirt and cloak were in tatters and he was bleeding from a plethora of scratches.

'Sigh, I really need to get a handle on my new abilities.' Tuck got the feeling that killing that Titan MonoOwl and getting out of here was not meant to be as hard as it ended up being.

He thought back on how he got here.

***

Altair Bashtuck, known as Tuck to all but his family, watched the rain pour while the waitress did the same for his coffee.

"Never seen you around these parts, mister..." She prompted. Tuck looked up at her, despite the best years being behind her she was pretty. Tuck smiled at her but his mind was on his trip.

"Tuck, everybody calls me that." he replied. She smiled and pointed to her badge.

"Name's Vanessa, my friends call me Ness, for short." she said. It was time to leave and make the next leg.

"Nice to meet you Ms. Vanessa, can I get my bill please, I've got to go." Tuck replied. Vanessa's smile faltered before she nodded and headed back to the kitchen. Tuck noticed her distress and replayed the half-listened to conversation. It took him a moment to realise his faux pas, he should have called her "Ness" and explained his hurry. Tuck wanted to kick himself, since returning from his last tour of duty the year before, he had all the social grace of a bull in a China shop.

'Maybe it's for the best, I'm sure she has better things to do than teach me social graces.' Tuck paid his bill and walked out to his rig through the pouring rain. The Diner had been a welcome respite as he drove cross country through the night to deliver supplies to a number of out of the way settlements. The heavy rains had caused a landslide washing out the direct route, but by the time they fixed it his most expensive cargo, meat and vegetables, would have spoiled. Tuck was still an independent, not yet a slave to one of the corporations but he couldn't afford the loss, so he was taking a more circular route. Fortunately it wasn't the dead of winter because most of these roads would be impassable. Unfortunately he still never made it to his destination.

Tuck was a mere 10 minutes from the diner when a flash of lightning leapt from the sky down in front of his truck, it was as if a crack opened in the world in front of him. He smashed on the brakes before attempting to swerve around the flickering hole but it expanded for a moment, just in time for Tuck to drive through.

The truck was surrounded by swirling colours and powerful jolts of electricity while the dashboard and headlights went crazy. Even if Tuck was curious, leaving his cab seemed like a bad idea. Not that he could even if he wanted to, Tuck realised he couldn't move. He was frozen, stuck looking straight ahead but fully conscious.

This was hell.

Time passed, first it felt like days then it started to feel like weeks but Tuck was unaffected not a blink, no bodily functions not even sleep would come to him.

Staring unblinkingly at the riot of colours Tuck saw a familiar scene, his room over his sister's garage. With concentration, the image got clearer. Trying with all his might he got the scene to change. It moved through the house to his sister weeping. There was no sound but he was sure she had been told he was missing, maybe presumed dead. Everything Tuck saw was in realtime, his control of what he saw grew and although he felt like he was like a ghost haunting the ones he loved, being a helpless observer was easier than just letting go. While attending his own funeral was horrific, seeing his nephews grow from boys to young men was heartwarming even if he couldn't offer them the advice his father had given him.

Watching the boys go off to college and return fully grown with families of their own brought great joy. But watching as his sister kept ageing; a grey hair there, a wrinkle here; until she was an old woman who finally breathed her last in a hospital bed surrounded by family. That sight brought anguish. Tuck struggled against his bonds but remained silent, the grief overwhelmed him but no tears could come. He stopped watching, letting the colours swirl around madly.

More years passed before curiosity got the better of him and he once again willed the colours to part. His nephew Peter was old and he had already missed how Sully, his other nephew, had died. Tuck followed Peter's life unil Peter passed from a heart attack. Not knowing his nephew's children, Tuck began watching the world in general.

He was disappointed by how things changed, because lasting change was seldom for the better. For every great new technology there was also some new hate group fanning the flames of division. Some of those groups did it simply for their own amusement. New wars constantly sprang up threatening to send man back to the stone age and if anyone investigated the cause it boiled down to greed. Tuck became numb watching the years churn pass.

After the second century he stopped paying attention to current affairs and went back to school. By now he had learned to read lips so starting from elementary he went straight to college, then he repeated college again, changing majors. Those bright lit rooms filled with hope and determination helped stave off madness. When the curriculum was mastered he did it all again in a different language.

Eventually man reached the stars, although those people had as much in common with Humans like Tuck as Tuck had with Chimpanzees. Either way Tuck was happy for humanity. He was attending a lecture on FTL engine design when he heard a voice, a woman's voice.

"I think I found the problem." The voice echoed.

Tuck, truck and all, were yanked out of the kaleidoscope of death and onto a placid mirror-like surface that reflected a perfect blue sky, both of which went on until the horizon. For the first time in nearly 800 years Tuck blinked. His whole body sagged, he was lost in sensations that he had been denied for so long. The smell of the cab, a breeze on his skin, the feeling of his clothing rubbing on his skin, taking a simple breath. It was all wonderful.

Although the ordeal seemed to have passed, Tuck still debated leaving the safety of his truck.

"Come out Altair Bashtuck, no harm will befall you here." The voice that called out to him was a different one but also female. Tuck braced himself as best as he could, he wasn't a coward by any means, his time in the Rangers would prove that but he was the first to admit to being out of his depth and this was the deep end.

He hopped out of the cab and turned to face the voices. 4 women, Goddess was the only word that came to mind, they towered over him and his 18 wheeler. Try as he might Tuck could not make out their facial features but they definitely had female forms, each made from different combinations of the primal elements.

"Good day ladies, please forgive my bad manners but I'm not sure about the etiquette of meeting Goddesses." Tuck said as he took an at ease stance.
"Am I dead?"

"You are not dead and your manners are good enough, at least you are not panicking." Said Goddess 1.

"He may not be panicking but I am. This is quite the blunder." Said Goddesses 3. "If you'd only checked that problem earlier…"

"You could have gotten off your butt and did it too." Said Goddess 2.

"Enough!" Goddess 1 exclaimed. "Assigning blame isn't important. Avoiding punishment is." Tuck had seen enough fuck ups to recognise them, they had made a mistake and he was now lost. He took a moment to compose his rage before deciding to risk speaking.

"Excuse me, ladies, can you not just send me back? I doubt time and space are an issue for beings like yourself." He said humbly with a little ass kissing for good measure. Losing his temper would get him nowhere.

"Unfortunately the life you had in your former world is over. You have been stuck in that spatial anomaly for centuries. Going back and resetting 800 years for a life that won't leave a ripple is not worth the effort." Goddess 1 told him.

He pushed away the what-ifs that threatened to drown him and let the news sink in.

'There is no going back.' He thought.

"What is to become of me?" Tuck asked. He didn't scream about his rights or demand to be sent back home, he knew that was a dead end. Human rights were a luxury even amongst humans. These goddesses obviously had immense power but they also had no drive to do more than the minimum, he hoped they wouldn't conclude the easiest way out was to simply kill him and move on. He needed to be careful where he pushed them.

"We should just kill him and forget this ever happened." Said Goddess 4 who had kept silent until now.

"We are trying not to get caught. Him dying before we change the report would be a red flag." Said Goddess 2. Tuck stored that useful piece of information away.

"We can't send him back to Earth or any comparable world... Shaards will do, it is a primitive world and very harsh but that is life." Goddess 1 said. Tuck continued to stand at ease, he understood he wasn't going to get a say in this, superiors making decisions for you was part of military life, but now he knew death wouldn't be instantaneous, he decided this is one of those places he should push them.

"Pardon me Goddesses, since my being here is an… error, I hope to gain some advantage to aid me in my new life." Tuck said aloud. The 4 Goddesses looked at him like he was a particularly ugly bug.

"Are you asking for a bribe?" Goddess 4 asked in an icy tone. Tuck saw the warning signs but didn't back down.

"Through no fault of my own I have been completely disenfranchised. Asking for knowledge of where I'm being sent or a way to protect myself. Those don't feel like bribes to me." Tuck made his statement in the same even tone he had adopted since he began speaking. He wouldn't let his anger affect his fate.

All 4 Goddesses seemed to find his reasoning sound.

"Fine. Altair Bashtuck we are sending you to a world of magic and superpowers which would you be interested in?" Tuck took a moment to think, Magic sounded awesome but in most of the fantasy books he read magic was just another subject, it only took dedication, superpowers on the other hand usually boiled down to luck. Tuck was confident in his dedication but was doubting his luck.

"I'll take the superpowers." Tuck told them. He decided to take the superpowers and learn Magic on his own later.

"So be it, on Shaards there are Titan Beasts, their breast bone is a type of crystal called a SoulGem. People can absorb these Gems to gain the Titan beast's memories and abilities and become a Champion. We'll make you a Champion along with basic knowledge of world of Shaards and it's languages."

"Ugh," said Goddess 2. "I don't want to go all the way to Shaards." Tuck was more than annoyed with her but continued to maintain a poker face.

"What if we just merge him with that Void Wyrm over there?" asked Goddess 4. All the Goddesses looked off in the distance at something Tuck couldn't see.

"You're right, it's within arm's reach and about to die. No one will miss it." Said Goddess 2.

"That is not a Titan Beast, and it is not native to Shaards." said Goddess 1.

"Neither is Altair Bashtuck. Besides, the Wyrm compares to the best of Titan beasts. And since it's almost as fast as a Kunpeng with a carrying capacity greater than a mountain tortoise Altair Bashtuck can continue his livelihood of moving goods as one of their Bagmen. I vote to give it to him." Goddess 3 said.

The Goddess somehow came to an agreement and one of them pulled a piece of darkness out of nowhere. It took Tuck a moment to realize the piece of darkness was alive. It looked like a snake if a snake could be made out of shadows and menace. Its purple eyes met his own and Tuck shivered, there was no intelligence there, just primal instinct.

With an errant flick of her hand the sinister looking shadow snake was thrown into Tuck. He had an unpleasant feeling of the void wyrm slithering around his soul before it disappeared into him.

'It is as if I've gained a limb I'd always had but had forgotten about.' Tuck thought before his muscles cramped and his body spasmed as he was transformed.

Tuck was right in his assessment, the Void Wyrm was all instinct. Eat, sleep, breed and survive, that was the Wyrm's entire life. It was the drive to breed that led him to challenge his sire for his territory but the younger Wyrm couldn't match the power of the elder Wyrm that had eaten suns before time was measured.

He had failed and awaited death as his sire closed in to finish him. Then the hand of a Goddess reached across the cosmos and flicked away his sire like the elder Wyrm was inconsequential. She gathered up young Void Wyrm, the creature that could coil around a planet was so small in her hand. It was brought to that serene space and merged with Tuck.

His mind settled, the man and the Wyrm were one and while his body remained human, Tuck could feel a lot had changed, he felt more level, more solid… confident.

"Well that came out great." Commented Goddess 2.

"We will exchange your items with their Shaards equivalent and send you on your way with a blessing of our basic knowledge of your new world. Good luck Altair Bashtuck." Goddess 1 said.

He was dismissed.

There was an explosion of light and Tuck was once again thrown into the kaleidoscope, but this time with his new senses he could perceive more. He was hurtling through space under the protection of the goddesses. After a long time He could see his destination coming up.

Shaards turned out to be a superstructure in space, a Dyson sphere. The entire structure had a perimeter wider than Earth's orbit around the sun. It was magnificent but it was not perfect.

As he got closer Tuck noticed that the entire structure was shattered. As if someone had put a cherry bomb into a watermelon and then tried to put all the pieces back together. He didn't know if it was the Goddesses' doing or just a result of natural gravitational forces, heck he didn't even know if there was a difference between the two, but somehow Shaards had been pulled back into a spherical shape but the cracks remained.

The scale was boggling even the smallest piece of Shaards was comparable to his old world, Shaards was millions of times bigger than earth and with his newfound power he wanted to see all of it.

It was then Tuck appeared in the Temple, his Truck gone but wooden boxes, barrels and sacks filled with items sat in a corner of the Temple. He was no longer wearing a polyester shirt, denim pants and sneakers but thick wool like shirt and pants with leather boots and fur cape.

That was where Tuck made the near fatal mistake of taking a look outside that almost cost him his life.

CHAPTER 2

Tuck sat on the floor of the temple contemplating his day when a question hit him.

'How did that MonoOwl know to attack me then?' He wondered, Tuck was suddenly certain that even at that moment, although he was within the protection of the Temple, the Titan MonoOwl watched him.

'All seeing eye.'
The knowledge floated to the forefront of his mind as if a long lost memory. This was the knowledge about the world one of the Goddess had promised him. Tuck decided this skill may be more overpowered than his Void Wyrm abilities.

Void Wyrm, he needed to stop thinking of himself as a human and start thinking that he was a Humanoid Void Wyrm. All the Wyrm's power and the Human intelligence to maximize it.

'What can I do?' he thought, turning his mind inward. His inherited instincts told him he could tunnel, reserve, attack, sense and hide.

'Ok but what do those abilities actually mean?'

Tuck had used the tunnel ability to get back to the Temple and dodge the Titan MonoOwl's first attack 'Tunneling' referred to space rather than earth.

'Awesome, I've got a teleport!"

Tuck quickly flickered about the Temple. It felt as natural as breathing to him but he noticed that he could stay in his tunnel.

The memories from the Void Wyrm, disregarded this as no big deal. It never paid attention to its surroundings once it was on its way somewhere, it would sleep until it arrived.

Tuck now found this fascinating while in the tunnel the world around him turned dull, less distinct and everything seemed to come to a stop.

'Maybe teleporting isn't the best comparison.' He thought. Tuck put out his hand to touch the temple wall but it passed right through it. He walked over to the altar to use its light source and checked for his shadow. His shadow would disappear as he entered his tunnel. He was both invisible and intangible, Tuck tested the ability, trying to move slowly across the room, he noticed his bubble squished space in front of him and stretched it out behind him. A personal warp bubble, so although the ability worked like a teleport over close short distances it was more of a hyper space bubble. That meant that over longer distances time would become a factor, of course those distances were Galactic, on the World of Shaards he could teleport freely.

'Let me rename that bubble my Wyrm hole.' Tuck thought to himself before chuckling at his own joke. He was quite amused by the thought of Wyrming through space. It sounded so much more fun than tunnelling.

'So what was a reserve?' He questioned. His instincts spoke to needing energy to move far and always having food saved in case of emergencies. Tuck analysed his inherited memories and found a near death scenario where the Void Wyrm had come out of it's tunnel between stars and didn't have enough energy to re-enter the tunnel. It had starved for months before finding a rogue asteroid to eat. Tuck's best explanation was that a Void Wyrm had a separate 'stomach' for storage. Since he knew the Void Wyrm to be a type of space time monster the chances of this 'stomach' being some form of pocket dimension was high.

Tuck turned his attention to the supplies in the Temple. With a thought space rippled, passing over the items and they were gone. At least no longer in the Temple, but he could feel them within him and could pull out any item he wished. He also noticed he could rearrange everything in that space as he saw fit. He had full control, his Instincts even told him items in there wouldn't decay.

'Neat, this could keep the name Reservoir.'

With that sorted he now needed to work out his attack. A large aperture opened, lept forward and closed like a blinking eye… No not a blinking eye, a snapping Maw. Tuck practised maneuvering his Maw and discovered he could attack from any angle and could open multiple Maws simultaneously.

Wondering where things he bit off would go Tuck sent his Maw outside and took a bite out of the ground. The rock wasn't his reservoir but a different space waiting to be 'digested'. Another surprise, just like with his Reservoir he gained knowledge about what was in this Maw. The Void Wyrm's instincts and the basic knowledge from the Goddesses combined to allow him to appraise things he should have no clue about. For example Tuck now knew this rock was high in iron content.

Tuck decided to keep the iron for trade and 'digested' the other minerals in the rock. Void Wyrms could eat anything. They literally broke things down into atoms and soaked up the energy. As the energy from the disinterested slag seeped into him Tuck felt better. All the cuts on him healed and aches and pains he'd started to live with faded, along with the gnawing hunger that was growing as he used his powers. Each gram of matter released an exponential amount of power that Tuck could feel being stored for future use. Punching holes in space was power intensive, Tuck decided he would look into a more passive way to feed himself in the future, but at the moment Tuck honestly had not felt this good since his teenage years. The lump of iron he had left back was moved into his reservoir without him having to bring it back into open space.

Tuck continued to mine for a while, he wanted to be in his best condition and have a decent sized pile of iron to trade.

After he had gathered enough and felt like a rockstar, it was time for him to understand Sense but he realised he was actually always using Sense. It stopped him from teleporting into a wall. But Tuck understood it could do much more, his journey to Shaards had shown him he could interpret data into visuals far beyond what his eyes could see.

As he tried to expand his Sense it felt like how people described an outer body experience, time slowed and Tuck's outlook expanded and he absorbed the information around him. He could even 'see' the Titan MonoOwl lazily circling, watching him through the Temple walls.

'That bastard needs to die.' Tuck thought. Putting actions to his thoughts a Maw opened in the MonoOwl's path and bit off it's head before another Maw snatched the rest of its body out of the air. Everything happened too quickly for the Titan MonoOwl to react although Tuck perceived the event in slow motion.

'Another unexpected benefit, this Spatial Awareness gives me a Time slow and my Wyrm hole gives me a Time stop.' Tuck revelled in his blessings but noticed his shortcomings. He couldn't interact with the world to take full advantage of the Time stop and hearing the Goddesses talking about that Kunpeng creature, he probably wasn't the fastest thing around.

Tuck dismantled the MonoOwl, keeping the parts that his new appraisal skill told him could be sold like the feathers, the eye, blood, meat and most importantly, the SoulGem. He disintegrated the rest, Tuck purposely did not think of that ability as 'digesting' since these contents included offal.

'I will consider that ability as Disintegrate.' he thought, as he tried to settle his queasy stomach.

Now Tuck needed to get past the flock of MonoOwls. They may be more docile with their overlord dead but he wasn't in a mood to test that.

"Let's try this hiding ability." Tuck said aloud.

A shadowy portal moved up his body leaving only his face exposed. It was as if he was in a borrow but this burrow was mobile. This ability was like a combination of his Maw and Wyrm hole. Like his Maw he could open several apertures at once, so his hands and feet could be out for attacking. Like his Wyrm hole he could hide in it but unlike his Wyrm hole he couldn't close it while he was inside but he could turn the aperture into a slit like the visor of a helmet.

'Alright I'll name this ability Shroud'.

So in all Tuck had a windfall of abilities. He had a Wyrm hole (Teleportation, Hyperspace, invisibility and intangibility), Spatial awareness (time slow), Maw (Attack, Disintegration and Healing), Reservoir (Storage and Preservation), Shroud (Hide and Stealth) and thanks to the Goddesses, Appraisal.

'I am overpowered as fuck and yet I almost died as soon as I got here.' Tuck thought.

"Fuck this place is dangerous." he whispered aloud.

Once again Tuck steeled his nerves and Wyrmed out of the Temple to the treeline below before using Shroud to make his escape.

Tuck revised his power list to include flight since his Shroud was basically letting him do just that. He didn't need to rely on the ground for his propulsion nor to change direction. He was also moving incredibly fast, instead of weeks it would take him days to reach the Human settlement without using his Wyrm hole.

Tuck weighed his options before concluding a field trip was necessary to help him refine his control of his abilities. Instincts were great but they were a poor substitute for skill. He needed to build up an ability memory just like he had a muscle memory.

CHAPTER 3

After escaping the mountain Tuck travelled cross country. It was a beautiful land. His surroundings reminded Tuck of similar forests he visited on Earth but while the flora reminded of his former world the fauna was alien and aggressive. This wasn't a peaceful land.

Magical beasts were the normal on Shaards. The bunnies could harden like statues, there were wolves that looked like living astro-turf, gazelles that flickered like a bad signal and so many more.

Every magical beast Tuck encountered was hostile. He witnessed a pack of creatures that resembled hares attacking a six legged green tiger who had snatched one their number.

Then there were the Titan Beasts.

Titan beasts could control the lesser of their species and they got their name from the ability to grow to enormous size with a corresponding power up. It was as if every pocket monster was secretly a Kaiju sentai villain waiting to enlarge and stomp on his ass.

And stomp they did.

Every day Tuck would seek out at least 1 Titan Beast to battle in an attempt to hone his abilities.

Tuck used every opportunity to experiment with his abilities attempting to master what he could do. Being completely unarmed helped Tuck to get very good very quickly.

More often than not, Tuck found his ability to flee his most useful skill. Being able to disengage any conflict enabled him to avoid panic especially since he couldn't win every confrontation.

Most battles with groups didn't favour him and some one-on-one battles came down to experience, which Tuck was now gaining.

He came across other surprises in his travels. The biggest one was that despite it being winter in most places, He found a few Valleys that were in full spring. Tuck's Spatial awareness detected geothermal activity that caused the conditions to be right for fruit trees to bloom. He had no idea if this was natural to this area but he took the opportunity to collect as many fruits as he could from these valleys of Eden as he referred to them.

The first valley was ruled by a pack of Grass wolves which were led by a Titan. Tuck quickly found himself out maneuvered and on the run, he had to change his tactics from battle to ambush to kill the pack. Claiming their den for his own that night, blocking the cave with a boulder so he could sleep.

When Tuck came across the second Eden valley, his Spatial Awareness allowed him to notice that this one lined up with his destination, and though he found it odd, paying attention to the Titan Shadow Lynx that had taken an interest in him was a bit more pressing as it began to stalk Tuck as soon as he entered the valley.

Tuck used the time the beast wasted to harvest the wheat like plants growing in the valley. When the Lynx finally pounced Tuck flickered to the side and punched it with all his formidable strength.

He had intended to test his physical abilities by using Spatial Awareness to slow down his perception of time. Unfortunately Tuck's counter attack made the Lynx not want a fair fight. It grew to the size of an elephant before sinking into its own shadow. While Tuck had no proof of what was going on he had read enough funny books to know he was in trouble.

From its refuge within the shadows the Titan Lynx attacked Tuck relentlessly from every angle. Despite pushing both his Spatial Awareness and Time slow to their limits and moving like greased lightning Tuck was still put on the back foot.

His physical abilities got more of a workout than he had planned for and as night was falling Tuck finally realised he had a major dilemma, just having shadows made the Titan Shadow Lynx unbeatable, the full dark of the night would make it a god.

Deciding discretion was the better part of valor, Tuck beat a retreat Wyrming away to safety.

'Being able to disengage is the only reason I'm still alive. Trying to go level for level like some Shonen protagonist is dumb.' He thought as he escaped. 'Once I'm done with this training I think I'll go the sniper or the assassin route.' Tuck concluded, he agreed with the Shadow Lynx's tactics; fair play was for idiots.

Only after getting miles away from the Shadow Lynx's Valley did Tuck decide to rest for the night. Since leaving the den Tuck had not found another area he felt safe enough to sleep. His enhanced physique allowed him to brave the cold and his disintegration of a few rocks or any beasts he defeated kept him healed and healthy but mental fatigue was setting in. Tuck stopped in the high branches of a tree to consider his next move. In the quiet of dusk he didn't even know when he drifted off into dreamless sleep.

***

A jolt awakened him, Tuck was in free fall.
His shroud activated automatically, arresting his fall and giving Tuck a chance to figure out his situation.

A troop of Gravity apes leapt about the branches of the tree Tuck had fallen asleep in. They were confused about the creature disappearing.

"One of those fucks kicked me out of the tree!" Tuck fumed.

Angry, ashamed and terrified; Tuck went berserk. Using his new completed fighting style Tuck attacked the entire Troop. Staying within his shroud, Maws snapped at his enemies from all directions. The panicked Gravity apes tried to scatter from their invisible attacker but none escaped.

Despite the perilous encounter Tuck was fortunate none of that troop were Titans. That kind of luck couldn't be depended on.

Tuck spent the next few hours figuring out how to maintain his shroud while unconscious, he would put himself high in the air and try to sleep in his shroud. When he failed the fall woke him, it felt similar to falling out of bed. When Tuck finally succeeded he awoke feeling refreshed. A solid night's sleep released tensions Tuck didn't even know were there.

After getting the hang of shroud sleeping Tuck's paranoia kicked in.

He decided for extra safety he would start to position the visor, the part of the shroud he could not close, under a tree branch so it would pass for a crack in the wood.

Having a safe place to sleep would make the Wilds of Shaards more tolerable. And although shroud sleeping was not as comfortable as a bed, rest was rest.

With this Tuck's travels became much smoother.

***

Tuck fell into a routine but he did not become slack. He travelled, avoiding magical beasts and only hunting Titan beasts. He had a dozen encounters thus far but he only achieved victory over the MonoOwl and a Grass Wolf Titan. Knowing how valuable SoulGems were, Tuck decided to stock up.

He no longer faced the Beasts head on, instead he employed assassination tactics. Still some of his encounters devolved into fights but Tuck was better prepared now.

Days later he neared the settlement. The rate of finding Titan beasts had steadily declined as he neared civilization. At what should be his last night in the wilds for awhile, Tuck took his usual precautions before going to sleep.

He awoke with the sounds of the forest and peaked out through his visor and was shocked to see the paws and tail of a familiar massive purple feline hanging down lazily from the branch he was sleeping under.

Tuck's old sparring partner the Titan Shadow Lynx.

It had probably been tracking him since their fight. Tuck realised he hadn't been very stealthy in his travels, going from one Eden valley to the next harvesting whatever he could find of value and fighting the Titan beasts he came across before Wyrming away.

He usually travelled in straight lines too, another mistake to fix. Since Tuck Wyrmed holed often, The Shadow Lynx thought nothing of it when Tuck's scent just ended. Little did it suspect Tuck was shrouded and sleeping under the branch.

Tuck had no doubt that if it had caught him napping he would have never woken up, so he returned the favour.

Three quick Wyrm holes: 1 to remove its brain, 2 removed its heart and the 3rd took the Lynx's SoulGem, leaving a perfect corpse which Tuck collected.

'This will make a fantastic fur coat.' Tuck concluded

Tuck walked out of the forest, there was a full day's march to the city's wall. The clear area between the Forest and the wall would be a kill zone for whatever ballistics the people of Shaards used. That whole area was blanketed in thick snow which Tuck used to stockpile water. He was able to remove the impurities and soon had over 1000 gallons of pure water saved.

This was meant for personal use, even in the more advanced world Tuck had come from clean water was not always available. Tuck also had plans for a luxurious bath, he already had a massive tree trunk in his Reservoir that he would hollow into a bathtub if he couldn't find one for sale.

It's not that Tuck needed a bath, he just wanted one. By putting his body into his Maw, Tuck could just disintegrate anything that wasn't him including sweat, grime and odour, but that wasn't refreshing, not like a bath.

Tuck was looking forward to the security and privacy of a room with a locked door, hot water and soap. Once he was able to sell some of the items he had, he would treat himself.

So far Shaards was a hard world and Tuck felt it was making him brittle.

CHAPTER 4

His first view of the Human settlement didn't do it justice, up close the wall was massive about 10 stories tall and hundreds of kilometres wide closing the gap between mountains. Running its length was a deep fissure nearly 300 metres wide that acted as a moat. Tuck walked up to the ledge opposite the closed gate and looked down. The chasm was a few kilometres deep with a glowing river slowly churning along.

"Shit is that lava?" Tuck whispered, completely astonished by the audacity of this city's builders.

"Ho over there!" A voice called from across the way.

Tuck looked up and saw… a Cowboy? He had the hat, the boots, and a revolver on his hip but the green Pancho he wore with the yellow bird embroidered on it reminded him more of the Tabard worn by the Musketeers. Tuck used his Spatial Awareness to get a better look at the hombre, beneath the poncho on his back the cowboy had a round shield and a cutlass. There were also many people dressed the same beyond the gate behind him where Tuck's physical eyes could not see.

"You must be cold, dressed like that." The cowboy continued. Tuck took in his own appearance. By this time his shirt and cloak were a memory and what remained of his pants barely protected his modesty.

"Well met, I am a Bagman called Tuck. I've come to trade and rest." Tuck introduced himself, pulling out a sack from his Reservoir before putting it back to emphasise his claim. In Shaards a Bagman was someone with supernatural storage whether through a magical device or a Champion ability. Bagmen and women were walking superstores and in a harsh world like this they were indispensable. The Cowboy spoke to someone Tuck couldn't see.

"Raise the bridge." A wide bridge swung up from below, coming perfectly level with the road from Tuck's side. He heard a bolt fire into place and took that as his cue to cross.

As soon as Tuck was across the bridge was immediately dropped. They were taking as few chances with Titan Beasts as possible. The cowboy and Tuck clasped forearms in greetings.

"Well met Tuck, my name is Armin. I hold the rank of Captain. Welcome to The Warren."

"Thanks." Tuck had expected an open space beyond the wall but he was in a large room. Tuck opened his Spatial Awareness wider to understand the geography of The Warren only to realise how apt its name was. What Tuck had thought was a guard wall was the facade of a massive building. He had entered on Level 3 of a multi-level city that extended out under the mountains and down into the earth. The Warren was a country all on its own.

Arnim talked to someone from his unit before returning to Tuck.

"Come on, I'll take you to Momma." He started maneuvering through passageways. If he was trying to disorient Tuck he was failing but he did not need to know that.

"I am assuming you're not speaking of your own mother." Tuck said. Arnim chuckled.

"Naw, she's the Militia's Bagwoman, Major Iskandar." He stopped and faced Tuck.

"It should go without saying that we, the Militia, get first pick on items being brought in. That's not going to be an issue, is it?" Arnim held Tuck's gaze as he waited for his reply.

Being hyper aware of his surroundings Tuck realised that Arnim had asked that question a bit loudly as they were walking through a very full lunchroom.

"That makes sense, you're the ones keeping everyone safe." Tuck replied easily. Arnim smiled and patted him on my shoulder. The conversation in the lunchroom picked back up and they continued their march to logistics.

They walked into a storage room that was buzzing with activity.

"The shipment from the green house should arrive within the hour and then you need to head to the farm to store this month's slaughter as well as the cheese, milk and butter." A tall thin man was consulting a thick ledger while following a short fat older woman with a jovial face and greying hair.

"Oh shut up Pete, can't you see that one of my favourite 'sons' has come to visit me?" Armin went over and enthusiastically hugged Major Iskandar aka 'Momma'.

"Hey Momma, brought someone to see you." She eyed Tuck up and down.

"Armin, you naughty boy, bringing me a stripper. I'm a respectable woman!" Everyone laughed, including Tuck. He knew how a nearly naked man walking this complex must look.

"My name is Tuck, I'm a Bagman, just came in out of the forest." Tuck introduced himself again. Momma became serious and smacked Armin across his lower back.

"You couldn't even offer him a blanket? Come this way lad. Let's get you some zes-root tea while we talk business. Pete reschedule my evening before joining us."

A few minutes later they were sitting in a warm cozy office. Tuck was wrapped in blankets and sipping on a hot beverage similar to ginger tea.

"Now, there is no way to look into someone else's inventory so we Bagmen have to go by our word. I'll have your oath that you won't sell SoulGems to anyone but me while you are in The Warren."

"You have it." Tuck replied.

"Good, that means you have SoulGems to sell. How many?" Tuck realised Major Iskandar had tricked him into revealing more than he may have wanted. Momma addressed Tuck's hesitation.

"Don't worry you won't be short changed. Our man Pete over here is a versatile Wizard and has a great appraisal magic tool."

"Why don't you go out and hunt the Titan beasts yourselves?" Tuck asked, they had the numbers and quite a few Champions.

"We do but it seems our current tracking squad is inept. Since they can't seem to differentiate between Titan and Magical beasts we tried brute forcing our hunts. On average we lost 6 Champions and 10 Gunmen for every SoulGem. That is not viable, so we are retraining our trackers now." Iskandar admitted. Tuck realised his training would be seen as suicide to others.

"Do you know your letters?" Iskandar asked, handing Tuck a clipboard. Her change in direction derailed his train of thought. It took him a moment to understand she was asking if he could read and write.

The sheet on the clipboard was divided into 2 columns. The larger one was headed 'item' and the smaller was headed 'amount'. With all the information the Goddesses had put into his head Tuck should not have doubted his ability to read but it was nice to have confirmation. Tuck quickly made up 2 lists, the first he was selling the second he was buying.

"I've noticed you haven't listed any SoulGems." Momma said while tapping the first list.

"Let's finish what we have before us first. You have shown yourselves as cunning twice already, I need to hold onto my leverage." Tuck said as he sipped his second cup of tea.

'Twice?'

Momma and Pete had a quick exchange of looks before both glared at Armin. Through his Spatial Awareness Tuck could see Armin who was behind him by the door squirm under their stares. They had rightfully come to the conclusion he had done something to put Tuck on his guard.

Momma's trick wouldn't seem bad if it was the first one, but following the trap in the dining hall the Militia seemed to favour manipulation. What Armin and Iskandar reminded Tuck was that the most dangerous creatures he would face wouldn't be Titan Beasts but other people.

Pete cleared his throat, indicating for them to begin. Tuck displayed the items he had listed and Pete appraised them.

Pete's appraisal magic tool was a pair of spectacles that he pushed energy through to determine something's worth. Since Pete's appraisals matched Tuck's own he decided not to haggle over the prices Momma offered. A few items in when Major Iskandar realised Tuck was just accepting her first offers she started over raising the price on everything.

The SoulGems she wanted kept her honest.

At the end of the assessment Major Iskandar introduced Tuck to the Warren's banking system.

In Shaards settlements had a barter system with each other and outsiders. Large cities like The Warren had a sophisticated internal banking network allowing for paper money called Grams based on metal weights. They had coins representing grams; nickel was 5 gram, tin was 10 gram, iron was 25 gram and steel 100 gram. Gold and silver were too precious to be coined since silver was valuable in magic insulation and gold in magic conductivity.

After the 100 gram steel coin came paper bills for 500 grams, 1 kilo (short for kilograms), the 2 kilo, 5 kilo and finally the 10 kilo.

When he left The Warren Tuck could turn in his bills for the weight they represented so he would have metal to trade at the next settlement he visited. It was a good system but not perfect. Tuck was sure The Warren wouldn't give out gold nor silver weights to anyone leaving the city.

Tuck purchased a shirt and pants (of course) but after that he bought containers in bulk. Bottles, baskets, bags, crates, wrapping paper and miles of twine; so he could package his findings in the future. Tuck would shop around the civilian section for a wider variety of clothing, toiletries, utensils and spices as well as things to sell at his next stop. He also had a personal project he needed to commission if he could find someone to make it.

Momma and Pete opened an account for him with the bank and deposited half of his earnings there, the other half they gave him in blocks of metals. Tuck took Tin, Nickel, Bronze, Steel, they even ponied up some Silver and Gold but he refused the Iron. Instead he exchanged his iron for the same weight in their more manageable blocks. Tuck was already wealthy by the time talk came back around to the SoulGems.

"Well now Tuck, I hope we can move on to your main attraction. How many SoulGems do you have?" Momma asked as a serving woman put sandwiches on the table. With a flourish of his hand, Tuck took out the SoulGem he got from the MonoOwl.

"Let's do this one at a time." he said. "You may wish to tell me how many you actually need, I already have enough funds to do what I want to do in town."

Pete put on his spectacles and began analysing the gem.
"A MonoOwl SoulGem!" he exclaimed, jumping to his feet. "The General must hear of this immediately."

"Sit and give me the analysis Pete, I'll meet with the General when I'm done here." Momma's voice was flat and Tuck got the feeling Pete had vexed her. As for Pete he looked abashed and sat down promptly.

"Y-yes Major Iskandar." he whispered. "The abilities to be gained from this SoulGem are the standard Strength, Speed, Reflexes, Endurance and Heightened Senses as well as the exceptional air manipulation and an All Seeing Eye." Pete concluded. Tuck thought Pete missed some abilities like slight precognition, sonic attacks and stealth but the more he thought about it the more he realised they would fall under the All seeing Eye or the Air manipulation, it was up to the user how much they could squeeze out of their skills.

Momma turned to Tuck .
"We need three SoulGems but we want as many as you can sell us." She said seriously. "We have an army to outfit. Anyone who makes it to Captain is supposed to be made into a Champion but we have 3 new Appointees awaiting their SoulGems."

Tuck put 5 more SoulGems on the table bringing the number to 6. 4 of them were from Titan Grass Wolves and 1 was from a Titan Juggernaut Rhino. He had about 5 more but that was none of her business.

"I want weapons. A crate filled with an equal number of revolvers and rifles. The holsters and belts needed to carry each weapon. Another 2 crates filled with ammunition. And finally a bullet mould for every gun." Tuck finished his list and let Momma think it over.

Armin whistled behind Tuck.
"You sure don't mess around."

Tuck had paid attention to the guns since he had arrived. They were magic tools not mechanical ones. They didn't use gunpowder for propulsion, instead the inside of the barrel was lined with magical runes that created a pulse of magnetic acceleration. They were railguns. The firing pins closed the circuit completing and activating the magic circles. They would be great sale items even if they would be next to useless against a Titan beast they could kill a magical one.

Momma turned to Pete for his assessment.

"The 4 Titan Grass Wolf SoulGems give the standard abilities plus the exceptional Light manipulation, I'm not so sure they compare to the MonoOwl." Pete told her. Again Tuck thought Pete missed the mark but this time he wasn't going to let Pete undersell his product so Tuck interrupted.

"Pete, you are disparaging a fantastic skill. Each of those 4 Grass wolves attacked me in completely different ways using the same skill. With Light manipulation a Titan Grass wolf made his pack invisible to ambush me. One of them had made illusions so it looked like it was attacking from everywhere while we battled. Another had gathered the sunlight and fired it at me in a beam. And last one pushed all the light away so it could attack me in absolute darkness, betting its life on its sharper senses. Plus I missed my killing strike against the one using illusions and it pulled in sunlight to close up the wound." Tuck said.

"Truly?" Pete was amazed.

"Truly. All Titan beasts are dangerous but with human imagination the skills the beasts have become truly terrifying." Momma added. "What's the last one Pete?" she asked. Pete looked carefully before answering.

"It's a Titan Juggernaut Rhino, aside from the usual skills it has the exceptional skill shield." Pete looked to Tuck to provide further insight.

"Not all standard abilities are equal, the strength you will get from the Juggernaut Rhino is next level. The one I got this SoulGem from used the shield ability to improve its charge, creating platforms to change direction and keeping itself safe when turning. Shield is a variation of the element known as force. If well trained it can be used to move and control things over a distance." Tuck informed them.

This had been one of the toughest beasts Tuck had fought. In the end he developed the technique he ended up using to kill the Shadow Lynx, creating a Wyrm hole and pulling out its brain and heart.

"All these beasts sound exceptional, how did you beat them all?" Pete asked.

"Those markings on him end in a vicious looking serpent on his back but I don't recognize it." Armin contributed. Tuck had forgotten about that. In this world Tattoos were the mark of your Soulbeast or the Rune tapestry of a mage's sect. Tuck's Army ranger tattoo had been erased when he arrived and Tuck had gained a Void Wyrm when the Goddesses granted him its power. If Tuck had remembered it was there he could have thrown a pelt over himself, he had lost the clothes he was carrying when the Goddesses traded him local ware for his own. He had gained cloth bolts rather than finished clothing. Sadly he walked in nearly naked. Of course that didn't mean Tuck needed to offer information.

"So, Major, do we have a deal?" Tuck asked, blatantly ignoring their curiosity. Iskandar got up and shook Tuck's hand.

"I'll ask you not to sell guns in The Warren as well." She said. Tuck agreed and that concluded their meeting.

Momma made sure Tuck got his items before heading off to her meetings.

Tuck changed into the shirt and pants he had just purchased before Armin gave him a drill on Gun safety. Tuck thought it surprised Armin how professional Tuck already was. When Tuck loaded the 6 shooter on his hip with 5 bullets and put the hammer down on the empty chamber Armin just shook his head.

Tuck put away his guns and was released into the general population. By now it was evening and Tuck was tired. The civilian areas were 12 ft high tunnels running parallel to each other. To get to the next street a traveller had to either go up or down a level where the streets ran perpendicular to the ones above and below them. Of course with Tuck's ability to Wyrm through space he could make shortcuts everywhere but he decided to use the roads and not attract attention.

Tuck went to an Inn called the Jaunty that Armin had recommended.

The Jaunty was on level 7, the first civilian level. Level 7 was basically a tourist trap. All of the inns and high-end stores were on this level.
Local living quarters were usually deeper.

Tuck walked in, found a table and inquired about a room and a meal, he people watched while he waited for the waitress to get back to him. People watching led Tuck to be astounded by the variety of hair and eye colours on display.

'Did mine change?' Tuck wondered, he was changing so rapidly in such a short period of time he wasn't sure, because of Tuck's healing and constant battles, the last 3 days of activity had made him more buff than he had been in the military.

'I needed a mirror to see how much I have changed since I got here. I hope I still recognise myself.' Tuck scratched his beard thinking.

The waitress returned and led him to the proprietor, a muscular older man who was balding but had a thick beard, Tuck noticed that the proprietor had a series of brands on his inner left arm. 3 Circles and 2 lines one of the lines had a diagonal slash through it, Tuck had seen these brands on a few other men on his way here but his appraisal ability did not seem to cover societal quirks.

"Greetings lad, the name is Boreson you wanna room for the night?" He shook Tuck's hand while asking.

"You can call me Tuck, I'll take your best for five days Mr. Boreson if it's available, and I would also like to ask a question."

"I like you already, 210 kilo, pay up front. Suite comes with a private bath and two meals a day. Ask your question." Tuck paid Boreson his money and then asked.

"What does the scars on your forearm mean?" Boreson gave Tuck a quizzical look before responding.

"You must come from further North than I thought not to know something so simple." Tuck immediately knew Boreson was in with the Militia. The recommendation from Arnim was one hint but how did Boreson know he came from the North? Tuck didn't react, he let Boreson continue.

"The circles represent my daughters and the lines represent my sons, the crossed line means one of my sons died before he reached adulthood. If you have any children I'd advise you to get marked so that the women will know what they're getting into. Liz show this man to Suite 1."

Liz showed Tuck to an apartment downstairs. Tuck thanked her and told her he'd take his meal in his room later that evening.

The Warren had no traditional windows below level 3 so this apartment had geometric patterns on the carpets and scenic tapestries on the walls. There were also indents in the wall where flowers were planted, the light crystals in the ceiling allowing for photosynthesis seemed to always be on. Tuck was pleasantly surprised when he noticed some movement on a few tapestries. He had no idea how it worked but they were ensorcelled so their scenes moved like visuals they represented.

Once alone Tuck stripped and went to the bathroom and as he had hoped there was a mirror in there.

'I am different but not drastically so.' Tuck examined himself, the man staring back at him could be a younger brother, if he had brothers. Tuck's father was Middle Eastern and his mother was African American, of Caribbean descent, looking at his reflection he could still see hints of both of them, his dad's hair and nose, his mom's lips, his complexion was somewhere between the two. The signs were everywhere, except his eyes. They were once a light brown like his mother's, now they were luminescent purple, the same colour as the Void Wyrm's eyes.

Tuck's body was covered in an ornate tattoo of the Void Wyrm the way it wrapped around to cover his shoulders, arms, legs and back reminded him of old Yakuza photos. Something told Tuck most Soulbeast markings didn't cover so much skin, maybe it had something to do with power. He'd need to see more to compare.

Before his transformation Tuck had already been tall around 6 foot 2 inches but before he was wide like a block. Now, rather than looking like a powerlifter or shot putter his physique was leaner, more like a runner or gymnast.

'I guess this is more appropriate to the world I'm in now.' he concluded.

Using his Maw Tuck did some manscaping, keeping his body hair neat, giving himself a Caesar haircut, shaping his beard into a box style and trimming his nails. He then indulged in a long hot bath.

***

Deep within The Warren a young man ran for all he was worth. News travelled fast and only the one who delivered it first got paid. He slid up to a corridor with 2 heavily armed guards.

"I need to speak to Mr. Wester now, he'll want to know this first." The guards were professional, teasing of others was beneath them, a simple frisk was all it took before one of the Guards delivered the young man to see Mr. Wester. Behind his back people called Mr. Wester the Weasel, his pinched face combined with his unscrupulous methods made the name well deserved.

Mr. Wester was in a meeting when he saw one of his guards open the door and wave at him. They knew how much he liked to have news first so it was no threat to them to interrupt him. Wester came out and saw the young man waiting nervously.

"Piro my boy, what news do you have for me?" Wester came close so they would not be overheard.

"Mr. Wester, I was up on the 5th level helping Momma move some things to earn a few coins when I see a man come in dressed in rags with the scariest snake I'd ever seen tattooed on his back. I heard him introduce himself as a Bagman before Momma took him back to her office. I made sure to stay close by and look busy. Marie was coming out after carrying in some sandwiches when I noticed he had like 4 maybe 5 SoulGems on the table." Piro rambled out. Wester's face split into a wide smile. This information was definitely worth a lot to the right people.

"Good work my boy. Did you get his name?" Do you know where he's staying?" Wester continued. Piro fought to remember for a moment.

"He said his name was Tuck, but I left as soon as I saw the SoulGems sir, I could find out where he is for you." Piro replied eager to please.

"No, don't stick your neck out any further, here take this." Wester gave Piro 2 kilo coins. The Young man's eyes lit up. The Weasel always paid his people well. Early on people tried to pass off bad information to get a better payday but after a few of them lost an arm and two legs and were left alive to beg for a living people stopped trying to lie to the Weasel. Having the best information network was hugely profitable.

"Thank you Mr. Wester." Piro was ecstatic.

"You know how to hide it so any ruffians don't get it all. Get out of here boy." Wester sent Piro on his way. While plotting his next step. He needed to put word out that he wanted info on this Bagman Tuck.

CHAPTER 5

Tuck awoke when someone entered the outer room. After his bath he had put on his shorts and sat on the bed to plan his shopping. He had no clue when he dozed off.

Tuck came out to see what they had brought for him. Being on the move for the last few days he had relied on his Void Wyrm ability to convert matter to energy and ate fruits occasionally. Tuck did not dare an open fire in the ferocious wilds and was looking forward to a cooked meal. Such little things were a luxury most people overlooked.

Delivering his meal was a gorgeous woman who was dressed in the uniform of the Jaunty. Her green hair and ruby red eyes caught him as striking. She was in the middle of unpacking a tray and pitcher when Tuck walked out and he was happy to note that she slowed down and eyed him in return.

"Thank you, is that dinner or breakfast, I was asleep." Tuck asked.

"Um… It's dinner, you checked in just after the noon meal." She replied while finishing her task. The moment grew long as she continued to stare.

"Joining me for dinner?" Tuck asked with what he hoped was a roguish grin. She blushed and closed her eyes to collect herself.

"My apologies, I was going to ask if you had any laundry you want done?" She replied.

"No, no laundry for me just yet. I've only got one shirt and pants right now. I need to go shopping before I have enough to launder. Just hope I can find my way." Tuck said, sitting down to his meal. Which looked like some form of pasta and steak Tuck wasn't sure which beast it was from but it smelled divine.

She stopped as she was leaving.

"I get off work in another hour. If you can spare 5 kilos I can show you about the levels, the best places to shop, which areas to avoid. Nothing ever closes in The Warren."

"I'd appreciate that, I'll be ready. Name is Tuck, by the way."

"Miriam." She smiled before closing the door. Tuck turned all his attention to the meal, savouring every flavour. Still the food felt like it was gone too soon.

Tuck left the Jaunty and waited outside until the end of Miriam's shift. Miriam came out and saw him waiting. Tuck studied her as she crossed the tunnel. Miriam was somewhere in her late 20s or early 30s, she was a tall woman at 5ft 11in, with smaller breasts, wide hips and a dazzling smile. She was built like an athlete and moved like a dancer. She joined him and they went down another level and found a busy crowd of people moving from store to store.

"This is one of the Merchant levels, you said you wanted clothes we can start at Ginty's." Tuck's tour started there, Miriam pointed out the best areas to get the things Tuck mentioned including a construction company that might be able to help him with his personal project.

Throughout the evening Tuck bought them various treats from the street vendors as well as extra for her to take home, Miriam protested that he was doing too much but Tuck insisted she take the food. They were both enjoying themselves, she laughed at his jokes and told a few good ones in return.

After finding all the areas he needed to visit Tuck insisted on walking Miriam home. She continued to speak about each level and pointed out the industrial elevators and the ramps that could be used for larger loads.

"This is my level, are you sure you can make it back?"

"Yes, I've got an immaculate sense of direction, here are your 5 kilos, you've shown me almost everything I need." Tuck told her and gave her the money.

"Almost? What area are you looking for I didn't cover?" Miriam was slightly incredulous. Her tour was very comprehensive.

"Well, I am a single man, in from the wilds and you haven't told me where I can find some female companionship. There must be places like that in this city." Miriam smiled knowingly.

"Usually that would be on the same level the Jaunty is on but it's winter, most of those girls aren't about. They have their regulars." Miriam told him.

"Ah well." Tuck sighed. Miriam gave him a long considering look.

"I've never done that kind of work, but I find you attractive and you are wealthy, if you would be ok with me, I could make arrangements to spend tomorrow night." She said. Tuck was flabbergasted, he did not see that coming and it obviously showed on his face.

"Of course, you probably want a younger woman... forget I mentioned it." Miriam retreated.

"No, I would be happy for the company." Tuck fumbled. Miriam smiled again, weighing his words.

"Ok then, tomorrow night. Good evening Tuck." Miriam said before walking away. She glanced back, saw him still watching and added a bit more swing in her hips for his viewing pleasure, which Tuck appreciated.

The society in this world seemed a bit more open about sex. Probably a mess of different factors that contributed to that outlook, the giant monsters outside were probably a big one.

Tuck pondered on that and other world differences while he went back up the levels to do business.

***

GrandMage Hizanko sat across from Mr Wester who was enjoying his glass of Tingle-water. She didn't like the shifty little man who had an appropriate nickname, he always looked like was up to something nefarious, not to mention how he ogled her Apprentice when he thought no one was looking. Disgusting. Wester was smart, he sold his information in two ways: you could pay per question, or you could pay a lower monthly fee and he delivered a missive filled with the week's pertinent information. On occasions where the information is time sensitive Wester made a personal appearance, like now.

"I believe you've kept me in suspense long enough, Mr Wester." GrandMage Hizanko stated flatly. Wester's eyes stopped roaming her office and focused on the stern elderly woman.

"There are whispers in the tunnels about how your prophecy went. 'Nothing comes from the north.' I believe that was the wording." Wester sipped his drink again, savoring both its taste and the GreatMage's annoyance before continuing.

"A Champion just entered The Warren, a Bagman with an unknown serpent Soulbeast. He came from the north." Wester returned to his drink, waiting for any follow up questions.

"You believe this Bagman has something to do with the prophecy?"

"Even if he doesn't, questioning him may reveal something... interesting." Wester replied. GreatMage Hizanko thought about it for a bit.

"I'd like to commission you to know what he does for the next few days, daily reports." She finally said. Wester rose from his seat and executed a decent bow.

"I look forward to working for you."

CHAPTER 6

At the Society of Crafts and Engineering Tuck commissioned a Hideaway, an apartment he could take with him. He was introduced to a young wiry man who was balding prematurely named Wiliat who was one of their engineers.

Wiliat showed Tuck blueprints for airships and caravans, both of which were mobile homes but far more complicated than what Tuck needed since his Hideaway didn't need mobility. Tuck explained to the engineer that he was a Bagman and this Hideaway was going to be buried so Tuck could rest when out in the wild. Wiliat really got into it, making suggestions about ventilation, sewage disposal, lighting and more.

Wiliat was able to work out an estimate so Tuck paid a deposit of half the amount and was told to come back in a few days.

Tuck stopped at the tannery and sold many of his furs. The Shadow Lynx's skin he left to get treated. He'd take it to a tailor to get a hooded cloak made.

His next destination was the agricultural and livestock area. There he sold off a lot of the meat he brought in with him. It turned out Titan beast meat was a delicacy and Tuck's fortune grew. On that same level Tuck also found people interested in the herbs he brought in to be used in potions.

Tuck's appraisal had told him which parts could be sold, but since arriving in Shaards Tuck still had not seen active magic so decided to buy a variety pack of potions out of curiosity. Their range of effects was impressive, healing, strength boost, speed boost, invisibility, intangibility, hunger suppression. There were also a variety of poisons of which Tuck also bought a wide selection.

Back on the main merchant level Tuck returned to Ginty's to buy an entire wardrobe including Winter and Hunting Gear. Afterwards he picked up a few things he thought necessary. Hunting knives, a battle axe, flint, rope, fishing wire, cooking utensils and a few other knit-knacks. On this level he also bought a lot of weapons and supplies wholesale.

Tuck's massive purchase earned the attention of the Branch head of the Merchant Association Director Opcide. She took the time to meet with him and they discussed how they could be of aid to each other. The Merchant Association spanned many cities and by joining, Tuck would get preferential rates. He also wouldn't have to run about selling things directly. Tuck didn't see a downside to them taking 5% for doing all the leg work. It was just that Tuck was finding he was enjoyed the leg work. He promised to think about the offer before leaving.

Finally Tuck returned to the Jaunty and his apartment. It was a good day, all of the shopping didn't put a dent in Tuck's wallet, he could rest on his laurels in the Warren but decided he would leave after his Hideaway was done. Despite the dangers, Shaards' wonders called to him.

The next day Tuck visited the Mage Assembly. They took up an entire level and were divided amongst 3 different sects. For a small fee he was able to browse their library. Tuck was curious about Magic but he found a few books early on that explained he would never be able to use it. Which was a shame since it turned out Tuck was literate in the runic magical language just like all the other languages on Shaards.

The reason Tuck would never be a Mage was because he was already a Champion. Everybody had a Magical core but for most people it was so weak it couldn't do anything, those people with a strong Magic Core are considered to have talent, with training and a sequence of Rune patterns painted across their body in a tapestry, these people could grow to manipulate any of the elements to various effects becoming a Mage.

By absorbing a SoulGem a person's Magic core changed into a mirror reflection of the Titan beast's SoulGem and the creature's effigy would appear on the person's body. That person then became a Champion. Mages had more versatility than Champions but anyone could become a Champion and they didn't require so much time to become powerful.

Tuck's feelings were complicated. He had thought he was gaming the system when he took the super power over magic and believed he could have the best of both worlds. Tuck agonised over his choice until he concluded that had he picked magic he would have died when that MonoOwl swooped to kill him. The instincts he gained from being a Void Wyrm saved him time and again.

Feeling better about his choice and now knowing he could not learn Magic, Tuck tried to find out the limitations of Magic, at some point of time he may be in conflict with a Mage. It turns out their greatest weakness was casting time, Magic worked like a programming language. Newer mages needed to chant and use hand motions but older mages basically had macros in the form of Rune tapestries over their bodies. Being able to cast powerful spells with just a gesture with the most dangerous mages just attacking with a thought.

'If I get in conflict with an Archmage I should just run and assassinate them later.' Tuck concluded.

Tuck also discovered that the runic language was nearly dead, it was so complicated it took nearly a lifetime to master it even with teachers to learn from. The fact that he could understand it perfectly was filed away for later.

He purchased some copies of maps and a variety of books on different subjects, including a few story books. As he travelled Tuck may find buyers interested in learning since he sincerely doubted every settlement is as well supplied as The Warren.

"Excuse me!" a gentle voice called out from the doorway Tuck had just passed. He stopped and turned to find a young woman dressed in Mage robes.

She stopped out of breath, leaning on her knees. Tuck took the time while she was catching her breath to study her. She was around 5ft 4in and looked young, probably just out of her teens. Her bright blue hair was cut into stylish bangs and her Mage robe was synced at the waist emphasising her large bosom. Finally she wore large circular glasses which made her eyes look bigger and more innocent.

Remembering what he had just read about runes Tuck used his Spatial Awareness to examine the young Mage again.

She blazed. Now he knew what to look for; he could see a complex pattern of interlocking runes covering her torso and right arm completely, with smaller rune patterns on her head, left arm and feet. Looking around the library at other mages he noticed they too had runes. Tuck knew there were 3 Sects in the Mage's Assembly and quickly differentiated their patterns.

Each Sect had their own tapestry but they seemed to be heading toward the same result and the higher your rank, the more your tapestry was complete.Tuck refocused on the woman in front of him.

"How can I help you miss?" He asked. She bounced to attention and spoke with bubbly energy. Tuck didn't think she meant to make her breasts jiggle like that but he was mesmerised all the same.

"Hi, are you the Bagman that just came in with out of season plants from the Bellphon forest from the North?" She asked.

"Yeah that's me, people call me Tuck." he introduced myself.

"Nice to meet you Tuck, I'm Adaline. Bagman Tuck I was told you found valleys out of season, can you spare the time to show me where they are on a map?" Adaline watched him intently as Tuck pretended to think over his schedule for the day.

"I don't know Adaline, I have a very busy schedule. What are you offering to make it worth my time?" he asked while keeping a serious expression.

Adaline stopped bouncing and closed her eyes to think. She tapped her chin while pouting cutely before replying.

"We have metals, we have potions and we have magic items. I'm sure we can find something that you want." she said.

"How about a date with you?" Tuck asked, stunning her for a moment. Adaline assessed him from head to toe.

"Dinner but not this evening." She agreed.

"Deal, let's make this quick, I have to meet with the craftsmen about my personal project." Tuck informed her.

"Thank you." she said, before grabbing him by the arm and dragging him away. Tuck noticed the other Mages cleared a path about her when they passed. Adaline was obviously someone of authority despite her young looking age, she had more of her Rune tapestry filled than most people Tuck had seen so far but that soon changed.

Their destination turned out to be a nearby laboratory.

"Masters I found him!" Adaline called out as she dragged Tuck into the room. The lab was filled with many elder Mages standing around a map table while even more younger Mages ran about doing tasks.

Adaline's master was a severe looking, tall old woman standing at the head of the Map table.

"So you are the young man in question. Come in. Junior Mages, we need the room please." The GreatMage announced. Adaline was surprised but bowed and obeyed, leaving with the rest. Tuck was curious what it was about. Imagine his shock when the 3 GreatMages attacked.

Ethereal chains sprang to life between the 3 Mages and Tuck. He found himself locked in place.

"Now you'll answer our questions or you'll suffer."

"The Warren is the furthest human colony to the north we know of, where did you come from?" One of the Mages asked.

"The fruits you were selling were out of season and fresh, where did you gather them." asked another Mage.

Tuck just hung there in the air, hearing them out for a moment. Then, as if he had flipped a switch Tuck stepped out of their hold. The GreatMages' eyes went wide. That wasn't supposed to be possible.

"I am going to be civil to you since you didn't try to kill me outright." Tuck said. To the Mage's perspective Tuck vanished from where he was and appeared next to the map table. The image of The Warren and the surrounding forest was still displayed. Tuck moved some flags to several valleys forming a straight line heading Northwards. Tuck stepped back and studied the Mages who were watching him warily. As they cautiously moved forward to see what he had marked he examined the fuller RuneTapestry the masters wore. They were the leaders from all three Sects, Adaline's teacher being one of them. By the time they reached the table he had their Rune tapestries memorised. He would paint them later and research the order in which the runes need to be placed at his leisure.

"What do these flags represent?" Asked Adaline's Master.

"At those points I found valleys, little gardens flourishing out of season, unexpectedly warm. I'm not from this area, I believed it to be natural but it seems I was wrong." Tuck replied.

"As for where I came from, Mages such as yourself should be educated enough to know the world isn't flat. If you go far enough North you find yourself in the South." he continued. Tuck began walking out of the lab before speaking once more over his shoulder. "I expect to be handsomely compensated for the rude reception." Tuck found Adaline and the other Junior Mages outside, while the Junior Mages crowded back in, Adaline grabbed Tuck and led him away. Once they were outside she gave him a card from her satchel.

"I'm not going to ask what that was all about, but this is a calling card, don't put it in your dimensional pocket. I'll contact you about our date." With that she ran back to the lab.

Tuck exited the institute, he had gotten lucky they weren't assassins. He needed some kind of passive forcefield, hopefully the Merchant guild sold something like that. Another stop to add to his tasks. Thinking of tasks, Tuck took out a notebook he had purchased and started to recreate the Rune tapestries he had just learned while walking to the Society of Crafts and Engineering. His list of things to do was growing longer and longer, but he was in no hurry.

***

As Adaline returned to the lab the masters were in discussion.

"What are we going to do about the Bagman, he's obviously something dangerous. We may have made an enemy." an old GreatMage named Andeton asked. Tuck shrugging off the dimension lock, sent shivers down their spines. They understood distance and walls meant little to someone capable of such a feat.

"He's willing to forget it if the compensation is good, so we'll just be sincere. How about we gift him a second life talisman?" Another GreatMage Rodert suggested.

"Everyone appreciates a second chance at life, that should ease any hard feelings." Said Great Mage Hizanko, Adaline's master.

"Now what are we going to do about this heating phenomenon? We all agree we need to investigate, but an expedition in winter will be treacherous. One way or another we will have to get either the Militia or the Clans involved." GreatMage Hizanko continued.

"The Militia takes too long to do anything." GreatMage Anderton complained. "Without evidence, getting them to take this seriously will be hard." he finished, GreatMage Rodert chimed in with a rebuttal.

"Once the Clans know of our suspicions they will focus on saving themselves and their wealth, making a unified effort near impossible." There was tense silence as everyone considered.

"We need them both. No, we need the entire council." GreatMage Hizanko said.

"They will accuse us of fear mongering." Rodert complained.

"What good is a reputation if everyone dies?" Hizanko concluded.

The rest of their day was spent trying to pull together as comprehensive a report as they could with the evidence they had.

CHAPTER 7

A few of the craftsmen in the Society had Titan abilities and together with Tuck they were able to make massive amounts of progress on the safe house in just one day.

Hours later Tuck returned to the Jaunty when he grew tired. He stopped to collect his meal and took it to his room.

Walking into the living room Tuck's heightened senses picked up the smell of a bitter concoction in a teacup. He had company. Tuck extended his Spatial Awareness and a smile stole across his face when he realised who it was.

Tuck entered the bathroom and leaned on the door, taking in the gorgeous sight of a naked lathered up beautiful woman.

Miriam froze when she noticed Tuck watching, her eyes wide, one hand going to her privates the other covering her breasts. Tuck smiled at her shyness but he never claimed to be gentlemen enough to turn away. Miriam blew out a huff of air and straightened up, her hands on hips, her attitude now defiant.

"This is me," Miriam said. "I know I'm long in the tooth, my breasts are small, I'm scarred and my body is hard but I'm all woman and I'm willing."

Tuck realised that aside from thinking she was old Miriam had some body image issues as well.

"I find you wonderfully beautiful even if you don't." he told her.

"Thank you Tuck, I'll try to make tonight memorable." Miriam gave him her best lascivious smile. "Could you pass me that cup of tea on the table?"
Tuck went back and brought her the tea. Miriam downed it in one gulp and made a sour face before handing him the empty cup.

"That looked unpleasant." Tuck remarked.
"Emphi-root, stops pregnancies, if your plan was to breed me and leave, you can think again, I'm not falling for that twice." Tuck placed the cup on the counter, Tuck had guessed Miriam had a kid, It was why he bought her extra food to carry home when she showed him about The Warren, he would ask her about her child later, right now Tuck had other things on his mind.

Tuck stripped and stepped into the bath with her but Miriam put her hand on his chest, stopping him from embracing her.

"I wish to make a few things clear, Tuck. As I said I'm not used to doing this for money. If you weren't a Bagman I still wouldn't consider this, but I'm desperate." Tuck chuckled, which made her frown.

"As a merchant I have to let you know admitting to being desperate puts you at a disadvantage in negotiations." She eased her arm allowing him to embrace her.

"I'm still going to take the chance. My daughter Jalissa has the talent and wants to learn but raising a mage isn't cheap. She just turned 6 seasons, in time for the next beginner class at the academy next week. it costs 40 kilo, I need 10 more and I am hoping you'd be willing to pay 20 kilo for tonight." Miriam looked at him with eyes filled with fear. Her negative self image was telling her she was charging too much.

Which she was.

20 Kilo was around $200, but considering money here was valued more like the old west, 20 Kilo would be more like $3600, Tuck's entire new wardrobe had cost less. Miriam saw him considering.

"I know it's a lot..." she stopped when Tuck pulled the money out of his reservoir and handed it to her. She looked from him to the money a few times, shocked that her plan worked. Miriam put the money in the overnight bag she had on the bath counter and turned back to Tuck.

Business concluded the rest of the evening was about pleasure.

***

It turned out Tuck's new found stamina extended to everything, He may have worn Miriam out but she seemed happy as she lay on his chest. Tuck was also content and sleeping soundly but his Spatial Awareness woke him suddenly as 5 men entered his apartment, oddly they came through the wall, not the door.

4 burly looking guys were led by a smaller weasel looking fellow. They walked out the stone wall holding hands like little kids on a field trip.

Tuck eased out of bed trying not to wake his partner, but Miriam was a light sleeper. She came awake and caught his tense demeanour. Tuck raised his finger to his lips and she nodded in understanding. Miriam leaned over to her overnight bag next to the bed and brought out a small handgun.

'I'll have to ask about that.' Tuck thought. 'I was told guns were reserved for Militia… maybe I already have my answer.' Tuck put together the pieces of the Miriam puzzle, her physique and scars wouldn't look out of place on a soldier. He had thought she moved like a dancer but he was mistaken, she moved like a fighter. Tuck added these details to the list of things he needed to look into.

Whomever Tuck's uninvited guests were, they were not going to get a warm welcome. He Wyrmed into the room and landed a haymaker on the one closest to the bed chamber. He didn't go full lethal on the invaders because the Militia may not appreciate it.

As Tuck suspected his assailants were all Champions. Three of them bound for him at incredible speeds but Tuck ducked and weaved effortlessly while paying attention to the Weasel looking guy still standing by the wall they entered through.

By now Miriam had thrown on her dress and came out of the bedroom. She goggled at the blurs of motion before noticing the downed assailant. Thinking quickly she took the unconscious man's belt to tie his arms behind his back before levelling her gun at the man by the wall.

He raised his hands, it seemed he had no intention of getting involved any further.

'Good.' Tuck thought, since he would talk, these other goons didn't need to stay conscious.

Tuck flicked his fingers 3 times and each thug went down holding his head and screaming. Tuck had used his Wyrm holes to flick their optic nerves. Once they were down he calmly walked passed, kicking each man unconscious. Tuck made his way to Miriam and her prisoner.

"Who might you be?" Tuck asked the smug, Weasel looking fuck.

"Just a man doing some business." Weasel face replied.

"His name is Wester, people call him the Weasel. He mainly sells information." Miriam supplied. Wester's eyes narrowed at the nickname.

"Good day to you too Lieutenant Miriam, so you stopped being a tracker to start doing Silkwork, what an interesting career shift."

"I resigned my commission." Miriam replied, she tried to hide it but his statement hurt her and Tuck was having none of it.

Tuck opened his palm and created a Wyrm hole. It looked like a bubble window, inside of the bubble was a beating heart.

Nothing got through Tuck's Wyrm hole that he didn't let through, no heat, no wind, no particulates and the only thing Tuck was allowing to pass was light so it took Wester a moment to recognize what he was seeing. The moment he recognised his own beating heart, the organ spasmed, missing a beat before racing at an incredible rate, the colour drained from Wester's face and Tuck spoke.

"I believe you owe my lady friend an apology for your insinuations. As an information broker I am sure you know the truth of her situation."

"Ms. Miriam I spoke in anger, please forgive me. I am so very sorry." Wester pleaded. Tuck would bet his fortune Wester was being the most sincere he had ever been. He may not have been sorry about what he said but he sure regretted pissing Tuck off.

"A-Are you a Seiryu?" Wester asked with a trembling voice. His question made Miriam gasp, her eyes locking on to the tattoo on Tuck's body.

"You don't get to ask me anything, you live for the privilege of answering my questions; why are you here and who sent you?" Tuck asked with unnerving calm, his fingers slowly closing around Wester's palpitating heart.

"The Clans want to do business with you. I've been asked to invite you to a gathering discreetly. The bruisers were sent in case you refused."

"Ah, I get it. I attacked the bruisers before you could get a word in and instead of speaking up you stood back to determine what you can learn about me to sell to whomever asks next. How close am I to the mark?"

"Dead center. I'm here to provide a service." Wester admitted.

"How much are you getting paid upon my delivery?" Tuck asked, curious about how much he was worth.

"140 Kilos total, I got half upfront and I get the next 70 when I get back." Wester told me.

"Hand over that 70 and head to your rendezvous, I'll follow with these mooks." Tuck said as he closed the Wyrm hole to Wester's chest. Wester handed over the bill fold and soaked into the wall. Tuck kept track of him as he moved between levels.

Tuck gathered up the fallen thugs in his Reservoir and got dressed. Miriam was watching him getting ready, her arms folded under her breast, her face nervous.

"Tuck, I swear this wasn't some spy thing." she began, but Tuck cut her protests short by gathering her in his arms and kissing her soundly. Feeling Miriam metaphorically melt into him was wonderful. Tuck stuffed the 70 kilos into the top of her dress.

"Don't skimp, get your daughter everything she needs for school.

When I get back tell me when you get another free night, I haven't had my fill of you yet." Tuck whispered to her. Miriam nodded while biting her bottom lip as Tuck Wyrmed away.

***

The heads of the Clans rarely met but they were in constant contact with each other. Given the chance, powerful Clans usually warred amongst themselves but in The Warren there were too many factions looking to pull them down. From the aloof Mage's Assembly and the rigid Society of Crafts and Engineering to the self righteous Militia and the especially greedy Merchant Association who loved money but hated monopolies that weren't their own. Of course the Clans agreed with the Merchant Association but since the monopolies in The Warren were their own, they loved them.

Each of the Clans Monopolised a key market; the Loreth Clan led The Alchemists, the Danub Clan controlled the banks, the Brambles controlled the farms and the Firths were dedicated to the control of information.

It was the Firths information network that prompted this gathering. The whispers around the Mages were disturbing but in this moment of looming crisis an unaffiliated Bagman appeared as if fate smiled on them.

Each Clan arrived with their guards, their heirs and a few servants. Now the Clan Heads sat at a U shaped table on a raised dais, their heirs sitting closely behind them. The servants and guards close at hand but out of sight.

For the last 20 minutes they sat facing the wall Wester and their guards had left through while discussing their plans and how to deal with the hapless Bagman when he arrived.

The wall the group faced rippled and Wester walked out of it. His nervousness was palpable and he was alone.

"Wester, where are the rest, what happened?" Headman Loreth demanded.

"I happened." A rumbling baritone came from behind the group. The members of the houses turned to look up at the devilishly handsome man with arresting purple eyes.

The heads of the houses stood up and faced him, unconsciously trying to mitigate some of the shift in power sitting below him represented.

The Bagman didn't move but a shadowy hole appeared and regurgitated the 4 unconscious Champion warriors.

None of the Clan's discussions had this scenario.

"Pay Mr. Wester and let him leave. We have business to discuss." Bagman Tuck commanded.

Tuck was having a grand time putting on this show of intimidation.

'These assholes thought to demand my presence like I worked for them already.' he thought. But for the first time Tuck was at a point where he had all he needed and then some. Tuck was finally in a position of power.

A servant paid Wester and he retreated through the wall.

"Ok folks, what do you want and what is it worth to me?"

"We need you to move a vast amount of resources quickly to a safehold of our choosing. You'll be paid handsomely." Headman Loreth stated.

"A sixth." Tuck's reply put confused looks on the faces of the Clans.

"I don't think we understand."

"I will do it for a sixth of whatever you want me to move, and I'm picking which sixth." Tuck's explanation set the room into an uproar.

"That's absurd!" Headwoman Danub exclaimed.

"We're offering a fair wage for reasonable work." She continued but Tuck shook my head.

"I don't need your money, I already have power and I'm not staying long enough to build influence. Resources on the other hand are always welcome. Take my deal or lose it all." Tuck turned to leave but stopped.

"Give me your calling card, I intend to leave soon, you'll need me to come back if you change your mind. Don't make me wait too long or my price will go up to a fifth." Tuck told the Headwoman.

She gave her card to a servant who handed the card to Tuck. With nothing left to say Tuck vanished.

The Families began quarrelling about what needed to be done to the upstart. It didn't take long for them to conclude he was right, they needed him but they had time to explore other options, the Mage Assembly had only called for a meeting to investigate the possible cataclysm they had no definitive proof yet.

Tuck listened to their talks while sitting in his Wyrm hole. What he learned wasn't encouraging.

CHAPTER 8

Adaline got to bed late the night before, Master Hizanko had ran Adaline and the other junior Mages ragged putting together what evidence they had to convince the council to help further their research.

Research seemed to be all that Adaline was good for as of late. She hadn't had she hadn't had a lover in the past four seasons. Objectively Adaline knew she was attractive. She was not only curvy but also had a vibrant outgoing personality that caused boys to think she was interested even when she wasn't. But all of her romantic options dried up when GreatMage Hizanko accepted her as an apprentice. Suddenly all of her 'would be' suitors evaporated like so much hot air.

Adaline wondered if they were scared off by her master's reputation or by the prospect that she herself would grow into a GreatMage.

If the male Mages were too intimidated to take a chance, it was their loss. Sadly Adaline seldomly got the opportunity to meet any Champions close to her age, and normal men, even soldiers avoided female Mages like the plague.

So it wasn't a surprise that even with all the hustle going on Adaline still went to bed with the handsome Bagman Tuck on her mind.

Seeing him standing in her bedroom doorway Adaline reached out to him.

"Kiss me handsome." She said groggily. The dream man in the doorway flickered and Adaline felt a real peck on her puckered lips.

"…!"

Her eyes flew open, she was wide awake now and the man smiling like the cat that ate the canary was no dream.

Her scream was followed by a bolt of lightning, which Tuck easily dodged. Adaline's rush to get up got her caught in her sheets before she tumbled out of her bed in a heap. Tuck maintained a good poker face, knowing he was in the wrong.

"Are you ok, do you need a hand?" He asked.

"Yes please." Came Adaline's quiet voice. Together they got Adaline free in short order. Cooler heads allowed for civil conversation.

"Can I assume you are not here to attack me?" Adaline asked as she donned her bathrobe, although it was in her head she felt more secure wearing her bathrobe over her light nightgown.

"Yes, that is a safe bet." Tuck replied, again his poker face was firmly in place.

"Why ARE you here?" Adaline asked the most crucial question even if it wasn't the one she wanted the answer to the most.

"I needed to talk to you about something. I was leaving you a note when you asked me to kiss you. I couldn't resist." Tuck's poker face finally cracked under the weight of his shit eating grin. Adaline was tempted to punch him.

"How did you even get past all the magical wards?"

"I have my ways. Can you talk now or…"

"No, I have a busy morning. I'll meet you at Advaar's for lunch."

'Making him wait will be a good punishment.' Adaline thought as she headed for her shower.

***

Tuck left, still smiling. He returned to his apartment but Miriam had gone, so after a shower and breakfast he went back to the Library.

Tuck was thinking he may be able to be an Enchanter. With his Maw he could do very fine etchings and he did have understanding of the Rune language of magic. Tuck's research confirmed his theory. He just needed gold to create the circuits and energy crystals to power the enchantments.

Once again the gift of knowledge the Goddesses gave him was proving the most overpowered thing about him. Rune magic had 27 marks that could be layered to make complicated glyphs of infinite possibility. Enchanters were usually old because it took a lifetime to master the Rune language. Tuck was benefitting from the Goddesses' biases.
'If a human could learn it, it is obviously basic knowledge.'

Tuck inspected the few enchanted items in his Reservoir including the guns he had purchased. Rather than experiment with a new enchantment he would try copying one that already worked.

Most enchanters were mages, they embedded rune enchings inside an item to make an enchantment. Thanks to his Spatial Awareness Tuck could look through the material and see these runes as clear as day so he had his pick of enchantments to choose from. He decided on the enchantment found in lanterns.

Since Tuck's Maw bypassed space he was able to duplicate what Mage Enchanters did by biting rune inscriptions inside an object, in this case a steel ring, he then injected the space with gold before hollowing out another space for an energy crystal. The inscription translated to 'TAKE ENERGY AND GENERATE LIGHT BUT NO HEAT.'

The ring lit up and so did Tuck's face. Descriptions in the library had made it seem as if even the most simple enchantments took a long time, but that had taken Tuck moments and his inscriptions were microscopic but very accurate. He could do this at a master level. Despite his superpowers Tuck had been sad that he couldn't be a Mage but being an enchanter would do.

Removing the enchantment was as simple as separating the gold from the steel.

Tuck had already bought a variety of items both magical and mundane. The price difference was staggering. From now on he would be able to buy mundane and sell magical, while pocketing the difference.

The largest expense for a beginner enchanter was getting Enchanting Manuals. The Merchant Association bought and sold them for high prices. So most young enchanters began with what their masters had taught them and built their library over time. Tuck on the other hand had both Spatial Awareness and Appraisal. He first went through his Reservoir to learn which enchantment had what effect, building a wide repertoire of enchantments he could replicate. He continued to find and add Enchantments from his surroundings and was always on the lookout for new ones.

Tuck spent the rest of his morning working out a maker's mark, he decided on a Serpent chasing its own tail in a circle, similar to his old world's Ouroboros. He would need to talk to the Merchant Association leader Director Opcide again to register himself but that would have to wait. It was heading towards midday so Tuck made his way to Advaar's to wait for Adaline's arrival.

***

Advaar's was a quality place in one of the larger tunnels of level 7. In front of the establishment was a fish pond which pulled double duty of providing fresh fish but also separated the clientele from the foot traffic. The entire side wall of Advaar's was a series of shutters that were opened up to allow patrons to look over the pond and watch passerbys.

Tuck got one of those outer wall tables far from the entrance and ordered a fruit wine while he waited. Adaline arrived with the lunch hour rush. Tuck waved to her and she joined him, they put in their orders and once the waiter left Adaline got down to business.

Adaline put a small jade talisman on the table.
"This is a 'SecondLife Talisman' drip your blood on it and it takes one lethal hit for you before breaking. The masters said they offended you and sent this as compensation. I have no idea what they did but it must have been pretty bad, nobody gives these away." Tuck accepted the item, he realised it wasn't an enchanted item but solidified magic. He couldn't duplicate this item. Tuck stored it away.

"Ok Tuck, what is it you wanted to talk about?" Adaline continued.

Tuck took out a SilencePyramid and put it on the table. The noise around them disappeared. He then put his elbows on the table and covered his mouth before he began speaking.

"I want to talk about the cataclysm you Mages foresee coming to The Warren." He said. Adaline's eyes opened in shock before she schooled her face and also covered her mouth to reply.

"How do you know about that?" she asked.

"I was approached by the Clans, they wanted help evacuating with their riches."

"Blast them all to hell, this isn't the time for selfishness. Sigh, fine. Long story short, We did a prophecy that showed nothing, which was disturbing but then warned that nothing comes from the North." she informed him. Tuck sat back and absorbed the information, that is why the GreatMages attacked him, he came from the North.

"Prophecies are unreliable, the act of looking changes them." Tuck pointed out.

"Good, we hope to change it." Adaline said emphatically. "The masters said you told them where they could find hot spots outside of The Warren. We started checking records of the temperature in The Warren and we found that temperatures are rising at an alarming rate. We sit on a Caldera Tuck, we have an elaborate system to keep us cozy but records show we are only using it at half strength. It is the dead of winter, Tuck. Winter in this region is harsh, we should be struggling to keep ourselves warm.

"I see, the Volcano is active but not volatile, so is it about to erupt?"

"That's what is weird, the lava hasn't risen, so there is no pressure build up. We get our power from the steam to run The Warren, energy crystals also form in the vents, we study the Volcano and the lake constantly, major changes don't go unnoticed. Does lava just get hotter?"

At this point the waiter returned with their drinks, Tuck deactivated the device and turned his attention to the people walking by. Surprisingly he saw a familiar face. He used a Maw to whisper.

"Hi Miriam, join me for lunch." Miriam was pushing a cart of school supplies with a little girl happily tagging along. Hearing Tuck's voice from out of nowhere Miriam spun about until she found him waving in the restaurant sitting with a beautiful Mage. Here she was tired and sweaty with her daughter. The last thing she wanted was to be compared to Tuck's other lover.

"Mommy, who's that?" Her daughter asked.

"That's my friend Tuck."

"Oh! Let's go." Jalissa grabbed Miriam's arm and started to pull her towards the restaurant. Miriam was about to protest about the cart when it disappeared into one of Tuck's apertures. Now she had to go, even if it was just to get her stuff.

The host of the restaurant had noted the interaction between Tuck and Miriam so he escorted her to the table and pulled her chair. Jalissa had run ahead and claimed the chair beside Tuck.

"Hi Mr Tuck."

"Hello Jalissa."

"You know my name?"

"Your mommy talks about you alot.

"She told me about you too, she called you my benny fracture."

"Benefactor, yes."

"Ben-e-fact-or… mommy says that means you are helping me get to my dreams."

"I helped so your Mom could send you to be a Mage, you like magic right?"

"Yes! Mages are the best!"

"In that case let me introduce you to my friend Adaline, she is a Mage in the Halceon Sect like you want to be." Jalissa's eyes couldn't get any bigger. She turned all of her attention to Adaline.

"I just finished enrolling in the academy. Momma and I did all of our shopping for the first year." At this point Miriam was seated. Tuck once again made introductions.

"Adaline this is Miriam, my friend and Jalissa's mother. Miriam this is Adaline, she is also my friend." The ladies greeted each other, Adaline gave Tuck a knowing look before ignoring him to engage in conversation with Jalissa.

The waiter took the new orders and left them but the conversation stayed light, Tuck learned that the magical Academy was a boarding school and Miriam and Jalissa wouldn't see each other for a year. He also found out that parents had to pay for the first 4 years of the Academy and then the children would be tested to see if one of the 3 Sects would take them. If accepted they would get their first Rune in their body tapestry. The waiter finally delivered the food.

Tuck reactivated the silencer and picked up the heavier topic.

"So Adaline, the heat is rising but the Volcano is not about to erupt?" Adaline was taken aback by Tuck's trust in Miriam. She wasn't expecting that. She looked at the other woman before she continued.

"It doesn't seem so but things are getting steadily hotter if it stays that way when winter ends The Warren will turn into an oven. The path you followed gives us some clues, we need to follow it as far as we can to find out what is causing the problem. But we need help."

"What do you need to do your research?"

"Truly we only need recording equipment but outside is so dangerous we need an expedition to get us there. That is why we called for the council to meet. We need the Clans, the Merchants and the Militia to aid us. The sooner we can find the cause, the sooner we can take action." Miriam listened closely while Jalissa ignored them for her food. Tuck mulled things over for a bit before speaking again.

"I can get you where you need to go safely and quickly, but only you. Your masters did not make a good first impression. How long will it take before you can move?" Again Adaline was on the back foot, things were progressing quickly. She had seen how Tuck had left her room, he was probably a speed type of Champion, he may even be a legendary Spatial type. Jalissa had been staying out of the conversation. She was a very well mannered little girl, the ice cream was helping too but now she heard bad news she spoke up.

"Aww, Mr. Tuck you're leaving? I start the academy in a few days. I won't be seeing mommy for a while. I was hoping we could become friends."

"Oh Jalissa, we are fast friends. In fact, no more calling me 'Mr. Tuck'. 'Tuck' is part of my Clan name of Bashtuck. The name my mother gave me was Altair. You can call me Altair, nobody else in The Warren can do that." At first Jalissa was very happy but a quick glance at her mother changed her mind.

"If mommy can't call you Altair then I won't either." Miriam was aghast at Jalissa's willfulness.

"Jalissa! I raised you better than that, you are being rude." Both Miriam and Adaline had been listening intensely to the exchange. Tuck was a mystery to them, both women were stunned that he had a Clan name.

"No Miriam, that's fair. Ok your mommy can use my name too." Tuck countered.

"Don't think you can leave me out Altair of Clan Bashtuck." Said Adaline. Tuck was about to counter her but she carried on. "I need to talk to my master to get permission to leave with you, I'll contact you and we can meet tomorrow, is that Ok?" Adaline asked as she rose to leave.

"Perfectly, I have a few things that need finishing up." Tuck replied.

Adaline left. Her master would take some convincing. Once she was gone Tuck handed Miriam a satchel.

"All of your things are in there including the cart." Tuck said. Miriam took the bag looking at it with awe. A Carry-All bag, she hadn't seen one since she left in the Militia.

"Drip your blood on the emblem to lock it to you. There's a second bag in there for Jalissa to take to school as well as a two-way mirror so you two can stay in contact while she studies."

"Tuck, this is too much." Miriam said, her debt to Tuck was already high. She had sold her body to him to earn 20 Kilo, but he had given her 70 Kilo after that. A Carry-All bag started at 100 Kilo for the cheapest and he had just given her 2 with owner locks, definitely not the cheap ones.

"You are supposed to call me Altair. Don't you want them?" Tuck corrected Miriam before he questioned her innocently.

"Of course I do."Miriam replied, more than a little flustered.

"Are you afraid of what I'll want in return?" Tuck asked. Miriam studied Tuck's face. It was obvious he wanted her, although she couldn't figure out why. Since Heric passed very few men offered her a contract but none wanted to include benefits for her daughter.

Boreson took her aside and explained that men didn't want to pay for a child not their own but Miriam wasn't having it. In the short time she knew him Tuck seemed different, he had willingly given to Miriam's child even before he knew her name, Miriam made up her mind.

"If you plan to contract me Altair, I'll accept under the condition you'll keep supporting my daughter until she is accepted by a Sect or, should she fail that, until she reaches her 20th season."

"Deal." Tuck said. He had no idea what her version of contract meant but a trip to the library would clear it up.

"Can we wait to enforce the contract after Jalissa starts school. I'd like to spend the next few days with her."

"That will be fine as you heard Adaline and I need to make a trip for a few days. We'll be back next week."

Miriam and Jalissa left, Tuck paid the bill and headed off to a busy evening.

CHAPTER 9

Tuck's first stop was the Society of Crafts and Engineering to collect his finished Hideaway. The end result of everyone's hard work was a hexagonal tower 30ft in diameter and 40ft high. There were no windows but was designed to be a self contained ecosystem powered by energy crystals. The tower had 4 floors, each room had an 8ft ceiling. Floor 1 was the entry and work areas, floor 2 was the kitchen and greenhouse, floor 3 was the living and training area, with the final floor being the bedrooms and showers. There was a lavatory on each level too.

Tuck paid what was owed and pulled the entire structure into his Reservoir. He then started etching protections into the structure of the building when he was done his Hideaway tower would be a fortress. Enchantments would allow him to enhance the mundane systems, removing the amount of service the Hideaway would need. He could also add new features as long as he knew the Enchantments for them.

With his new home secured, Tuck visited the Merchant Association. Both the Mages and the Clans had approached him so callously because he had no backing. If Tuck continued to stand alone he would need to struggle to find footing wherever he went.

Once again Director Opcide received him warmly. Tuck joined the Association. After filling out the paperwork Director Opcide was surprised to find out Tuck had a Clan name, he told her his Clan was defunct, destroyed by a Titan no one could stand against. Director Opcide nodded in understanding, he didn't go into detail that the beast was time itself.

"Director Opcide, I will speak frankly with you. I'm not willing to work my way up over time to a position of trust. I know I have a degree of freedom because I am a Bagman but how do I spin that into an executive position within the organisation?"

"Mr Tuck the Merchant Association has a staggering breadth across the Shaards. Each branch you come to is a franchise united but individual, the majority of Association members are just sales people who pay a tithe in exchange for umbrella protection, this includes our Bagmen. If you wish for a higher position you either have to form your own branch or provide a highly skilled service to the association at a preferred rate."

"I am an Enchanter, would that skill be enough?"

"Truly? I heard you were a Champion not a Mage." Opcide said to Tuck with a skeptical look.

"You heard correctly, my ability allows for me to be a Master Enchanter, let me prove it to you, an Enchanter's worth is in their speed and range of enchantments." Tuck offered, this was a chance to impress the Merchant Association.

"Okay, Merchant Association Enchanters are required to enchant 10 items from an approved list for the Association every month. The mundane items, gold and power crystals are provided, the only cost to you is your skill and time. After meeting their quota any other enchanted items you want to sell you will get full price for. As well as VIP status at any branch you visit. Of course if the Association puts a more complicated enchantment list like Golems or a request that means you have to travel like wards additional rewards would be offered." Tuck nodded his understanding.

"Let's test you out with 10 various items that have been on the list for a while. I'm sad to admit we do have a backlog to clear." Director Opcide put 10 items on the table, a list of what enchantments needed to be put on them, along with gold and crystals. "A master enchanter could do these in a few hours, I'll time you."

"That sounds useful." Tuck said. He then amazed Director Opcide by enchanting 9 of the items in minutes adding his recently registered maker's mark, a tiny Ouroboros symbol, on each. The last item, a Signet-ring with the engraving of Clan Danub, Tuck held in his hand and showed Opcide.

"Director Opcide, I cannot make this into a Spatial-Ring." Tuck had learned 3 different dimensional pocket enchantments from 3 different quality Carry-All bags but he had not yet worked out how to make spatial rings which were many times smaller but had a dimensional pocket magnatudes bigger. Of course Tuck wouldn't admit that.

When he figured it out or found a spatial ring to learn from he would need the Merchant Association to believe he had the skill all along. "I'm in talks with the Clans to move items for them, but if I make this I lose my bargaining power." Tuck told a half truth to cover himself. Director Opcide smiled in understanding.

"Of course, no more Spatial-rings until your negotiations are through, you never know where they may end up." Despite not getting the last item enchanted, Opcide realised what a prodigy she had on her hands. She registered Tuck as a Master Enchanter and paid him to clear her backlog of enchantment requests and nearly 100 other complicated enchantments that other branches of the association desperately needed. If she had to wait on the other Enchanters in the association to do them it would take years. There was nothing in that list beyond what Tuck could do. Some things took more creative thinking but since Tuck understood the Rune language he could solve these simple impediments.

While Tuck worked he asked Director Opcide what he wanted to know about contracts.

"Director Opcide I come from outside The Warren, there is a young woman I've taken as a lover who is willing to be contracted to me but I'm unsure what exactly that entails. Please explain what it means in detail." Tuck said. Director Opcide smiled at Tuck's naivete, she found it refreshing. She spoke after gathering her thoughts.

"There are many types of contacts but when it comes to sexual relationships there are only 3. Indentury, marriage and slavery.

Indentury is a contract between people of unequal statuses, a master and a servant.

This is the most common contract between lovers. The lover with the higher status, the master, pays a lump sum for the other, the servant, to the servant's family.

The master leads and provides while the servant follows and obeys. Either side can cancel the contract but if the servant does it they have to repay a percentage of what their family was given. In case of separation any children belong to the master's family. You can already see how this type of contract is a bit of a trap.

The key thing is the master can have many servants but the servants cannot have another master." Opcide informed him Tuck thought it sounded like an old timey marriage, mixed with a harem.

"Ok, so what is a marriage?" Tuck asked.

"Then the people in the contract would have to have similar statuses and either no gifts are given or gifts of equal value are exchanged."

"And slavery?"

"One of the people has no status at all, and no rights.

My mother always says 'Society is built on contracts'." Opcide told him. She had taken her mother's words to heart and became a Scribe.

"Tuck, unless your lover is a member of one of the Clans, a Champion or a Mage you should offer her a slave contract. Companionship is cheap. If she has no more to offer than that she will accept."

"Wouldn't you be insulted if your lover offered you a slave contract?" Tuck asked Director Opcide. She threw back her head and laughed.

"I've had 3 men sire all my children. All of them my slaves. I am a Mage, a Scribe and the head of a branch of the Merchant Association. There is no mortal man with enough power to offer me a slave contract. Even if I were 40 years younger the best a handsome beau like you could have offered me was a Marriage contract."

Other than learning about contracts Tuck also learned about the association itself, Opcide did not know the full scale of the Merchant Association. She rose up through The Pitt branch and was sent to take over The Warren branch nearly 20 seasons ago. Every branch has a small Transit gate and Communication Crystal Ball. Only for executive use. This allowed the branch managers and their staff to stay ahead of trends and developments. Escape threats and mobilise the Association's strike force.

With this magical array the entire Merchant Association would know who Enchanter and Bagman Altair Bashtuck was by the end of the day and nearly 100 of them would have a sample of his work.

There was also the Merchant fleet; individual captains who joined the Association to ensure they could find work.

Tuck concluded he had made a good choice in joining a world power.

After Tuck finished his Enchanting, Opcide offered to pen his contracts personally.

***

Later that night GreatMage Hizanko and Adaline sat in the GreatMage's office. Adaline had rushed back but got so busy she hadn't had time to talk to her master until now.

Of course Hizanko was against her precious apprentice running off with some stranger. She had intended to attack the upstart to see what he was made of but Adaline confided in her master that Tuck could manipulate space.

GreatMage Hizanko was one of those people who believed Champions to be inferior to Mages but even she wasn't confident against Space manipulation, after all it was a legendary skill.

"Sigh, you realise he just wants to get in your small clothes right?" Hizanko finally said.

"You are being too harsh, master. He is very direct, and he doesn't have to work so hard if that was his goal."

"Fine, fine, you obviously like him, so have your fun but I beg you to do your job well." Hizanko got up and went to a painting of a treasure trove hanging on the wall. She whispered an incantation and was able to reach into the painting and pull out a small chest. Hizanko removed a chain with 2 pendants, one red, the other blue. She took the blue pendant and put it on her desk, the other she left on the chain and walked around behind Adaline to put it around her neck.

"I don't care if you two are humping like bunnies, this NEVER comes off. It is a return amulet. It will bring the wearer to the other amulet, which I will keep here in my office. The Merchant Association finally sent one over, I had this on backorder forever it showed up at just the right time." Hizanko returned to her seat.

"Take all you need to record everything. The Warren council meets on the next First day so you have 6 days to go as far as you can to track this phenomenon. No matter what you find, return and report on First day."

"Yes master."

"Most of all my child, be careful. The wilds are unforgiving."

Adaline thanked her master and left to get prepared.

CHAPTER 10

Miriam was in her apartment where she sat with Tisa, her friend and Jalissa's paternal Aunt.

Tisa was a dressmaker and had a marriage contract with a ship Captain. The two lived next to Miriam and had 3 children, 2 boys and a girl. The eldest boy Cameron was 7, the second boy Tyrwell was 5 and the last child, their girl Patti was 3. With Jalissa always with her cousins they were close as siblings. Something Miriam was always thankful for.

Jalissa and Tisa's 3 children were playing a game while their mothers talked when there was a knock at the door and Jalissa ran to answer it.

Jalissa looked out to see Tuck waiting.

"Altair!" She exclaimed before glomping onto him with a hug. Taking Tuck by the hand she pulled him into the house.
"Everybody meet Mr Bashtuck, he's my friend."

"Hello everybody." Tuck said. He gave Jalissa a bag of cupcakes to share amongst her cousins.

"My, my, my. Mr Bashtuck, Miriam didn't mention how handsome you were. I am Tisa." Tisa gave Miriam a wink and reached out to shake Tuck's hand.

"Nice to meet you Ms Tisa everybody calls me Tuck."

"Tuck it is, I'll be with the children since you two have something to discuss." Tisa got up and went into the living room with the kids. Tuck waited until they were alone to hand Miriam the Indentureship contract.

"I was expecting a slave contract with our status differences. Thank you for not doing that to me." Miriam signed the contract right below Tuck's signature. The paper glowed and turned into two motes of lights and flew into each of them. Tuck became even more aware of Miriam's presence and she of his.

"From now on you are mine. My first wife. quit your job at the Jaunty." Tuck took out 1000 Kilo in bills. "Use that to pay off your bills and deposit the rest." Miriam took the money and put it into her new Carry-All bag.

"While I'm gone I want you to gather information for me on what is going on in the Warren. There is a saying where I'm from, 'Give a man a fish you feed him for a day. Teach a man to fish and you feed him for a lifetime.'" Miriam gave Tuck a curious look.

"It's a good saying, but what does that have to do with spying?" She asked. Tuck reached into his reservoir and pulled out a SoulGem.

"I'm about to teach you to fish. Shaards is a world about power. This SoulGem came from a Titan Shadow Lynx. It was one of my toughest opponents. It could literally move though shadows and control darkness. From my own experiences controlling space. I can influence time. So if you manage to master darkness, you may be able to influence light, your imagination is the only limit on your power. Absorb this now." Miriam teared up, she had wanted to be Champion all her life and now it was happening. In a rush of emotion she told Tuck her past.

Her father was a Champion in the Militia, Miriam learned tracking from him and was awed by his Mountain Ramm Soulbeast power. Miriam idolised her father, when she grew up she joined the Militia following in his footsteps.

Miriam was the best tracker the Militia had; some would say she was the only good tracker. Her C.O. Commander Lixor noticed the drop in successful hunts when she was on maternity leave but rather than revise the training of the other trackers he buried the details and conspired to keep Miriam where she was to keep the quota of SoulGems up.

When Jalissa was only 2 years old Miriam's mate Captain Heric died, suddenly Miriam needed to take a desk job. Lixor dangled the chance for promotion to Captain over her head for a full year. Wanting to be a Champion Miriam persevered but eventually she had enough and took her case up to Militia court.

When they also promised her 'soon', Miram resigned her commission in frustration. Boreson had been kind enough to offer her a job and treat her like one of his own daughters but the unreasonable treatment from the Militia still stung.

Miriam told Tuck as much as she dried her tears.

"That jackass Commander Lixor would see my daughter an orphan if I let him." she concluded. Tuck never met Lixor but he could see the similarities between his tactics and Captain Arnim's. The conversation with Major Iskandar revealed that the upper echelon was now aware of the issue, though he had no idea if anything was done about it.

"Well I don't need you helpless, nor weak, we're going to be travelling together while Jalissa is in school. I want to see as much of this world as I can."

"Understood. I will be a good and faithful first wife, and help rebuild the Bashtuck Clan." Miriam made that declaration with a ferocity Tuck had yet to see before. She then took up the SoulGem and began absorbing it. Tuck never saw someone become a Champion, he pulled both of them into his Maw just in case there was a phenomenon.

Miriam held the SoulGem up to her chest and it slowly soaked into her flesh. There was then a pulse of darkness and all of Miram cramped with pain. Her body transformed, more muscle, more pronounced curves, her breasts became fuller and a size larger. Everything about Miriam became more refined. Miram's body relaxed and when Tuck was sure it was all over he released his Maw.

Tlsa and the children were gathered around wide eyed. They all noticed the changes in Miriam, the kids all jumped on her.

"Mommy, you are so pretty."

"Aunty Miriam you've become a Champion?"

Miriam told the family she was now Tuck's woman. Word spread around the neighbourhood and a party started, Miriam was very popular in this sector and everyone celebrated into the night.

***

Tuck awoke with Miriam wrapped around him. They had carried Tisa and her children home and Miriam had asked her to keep Jalissa for the night. Miriam and Tuck went back to her apartment and made love until the early morning.

Tuck kissed Miriam good morning before getting dressed, she stayed in bed wrapped in the sheets and appreciated watching him get dressed. Tuck leaned in to kiss her again and give her some advice.

"Practice with your powers. You have your Shadow Lynx's understanding of your ability but with human imagination you will be able to do so much more." He told her.

"I can just imagine what you can do since you control space and time. I'll try my best to see what darkness can do." She replied.

"You are making me sound more powerful than I am, it is more like I have my own space that I push out to influence the world around me." Tuck smiled. Miriam looked him in the eye as she weighed her words before speaking.

"Altair, I've seen you pull out a pie, hours after it was baked. It was still steaming. You stopped time for it and if you can stop time in that space of yours you should be able to speed it up or even reverse it." Miriam was still studying Tuck's expression as she finished. "You control space and time." Tuck's face went slack, he was flabbergasted.

'Was she right?' Tuck closed his eyes and focused on the kitchen garden in his Hideaway which he kept in his Reservoir. There was light and water but only seeds. Tuck concentrated on moving the time in this part of his Reservoir, It felt like flexing a muscle and then things shifted. The seeds bloomed into vegetables and withered in a moment.

'Too much.' Tuck tried again, this time more gently and going the other way. The withered food became vibrant and lush once again. Tuck released his influence and the stasis time returned.

Tuck sat heavily on the edge of the bed and rubbed his face suddenly feeling cold. He could age somebody to death or return someone's youth. Could he undo catastrophic injuries? Could he resurrect the dead? What happened to the soul when he brought that person back?

It was overwhelming.

Miriam got up and hugged him. Raising his lowered head to her bosom. She had continued to study his reaction to her words and had seen the moment the realisation of how powerful he might be hit him.

"I've heard legends of you immortals going crazy with power and destroying themselves but I believe you can handle it Altair, you are not a good man, but you are a great one." Miriam said to Tuck.

"Why would you think me an immortal?" He asked.

"Are you not?" Tuck had no rebuttal, thanks to the Void Wyrm his memory went back millennia and because of the time rift he fell into Tuck was born centuries ago. His healing would most likely counter his ageing and if it didn't he could just enter his reservoir and turn back time. He could as well be immortal.

"Ok, so how did the other immortals fall?" Tuck asked, learning from his own mistakes had served him well, but if he could learn from the mistakes of others he would gain some wisdom.

"Pride, always hubris. Immortality is not invincibility. Be careful of that." Miriam told him before kissing his forehead.

"Are you feeling better now?" She asked. Tuck held her around her waist, pressed his lips against her breasts and blew out air to create indecent farty noises. Miriam laughed.

"Boobs make everything better." He laughed with her.

"Get going you fool." Miriam sent Tuck on his way with a fond smile.

CHAPTER 11

Tuck Wyrmed to the Jaunty and took a bath before he checked out. Adaline's call came while he was walking to the shopping plaza. The portrait on her calling card animated as she spoke through it.

"My master agreed and I am ready to go. Where should I meet you?"

Tuck decided there was no need to be subtle and appeared next to Adaline. She squeeked in surprise.

"Activate your magical defences, we'll be outside in a moment." Adaline did as she was told.

Tuck laid his hand on Adaline's shoulder and they were outside The Warren in a burnt out wasteland. Adaline did a spell that showed their location and looked to Tuck in amazement. They had travelled miles in the blink of an eye.

Tuck was more astonished how this valley had changed. What was a lush paradise was now burnt to ruin.

"Take your readings, we have 8 more of these that I know about. Then we'll be travelling more conventionally looking for more." Tuck took up watch, his Spatial Awareness extended and looking for threats but the magical beasts that frequented the valleys had fled the area. The frozen forest was looking more like spring had come.

Tuck noticed Adaline sweating. She had come out dressed for winter wearing a thick cloak and pants while Tuck had dressed more lightly. He was not underestimating how bad the weather could have been nor was he relying on his own ability to withstand the cold, he was however prepared this time around. Tuck had created for himself an environmental charm, the necklace he wore was enchanted to provide a thin layer of protection around his body. When it was cold it kept him warm, when it was warm it kept him cool and if it was wet it kept him dry.

Other than the environmental necklace Tuck also enchanted his belt to provide a force field so that he could survive attacks that got past his Spatial Awareness. After all it's the threats you don't see coming that end you.

His last enchanted items were his boots. His time as a Ranger taught him the importance of good boots, so their enchantments were for the sole purpose of comfort and durability; every step Tuck made felt like he was stepping into a deep shag rug and once he tied the laces they adjusted to fit him snugly like a second layer of skin.

"Altair." Adaline called to him, she insisted on using his first name now she knew it.

"I've finished my scans, there's only a few metres separating this valley from a pool of magma below." Adaline informed him as she fanned herself, sweat was dripping off her and her breathing was laboured.

"I have an environmental necklace that you can wear but you will have to take off that one, wearing 2 magic items in the same place interfere with each other." Tuck said to Adaline showing her his own necklace.

"I would love that but I can't, my master made me swear not to take this off not even when I was showering." She replied glumly. They were in the first valley and she was already miserable.

"If I had a circlet or a tiara I could put the enchantment on that." Tuck mused. Adaline was again surprised.

"Altair, you are an enchanter?"

"Yes, the piece you wear is one of my works." Tuck told her, he then showed her his maker's mark of a snake eating its tail on both necklaces. Adaline was delighted she couldn't wait to tease her master about this.

"I can craft a circlet with an energy crystal for you to enchant. But that can wait until tonight." Adaline stripped out of her clothes down to some shorts and a tank top. She put her clothes into her Carry-All bag and took out a towel.

"Let's head to the next one." She said with determination. Tuck was happy to see that Adaline was a trooper, he took her hand and they were at the next valley.

This valley was the same as the other. Burnt. It was the same for the other 6 in the last one they encountered the first set of magic beasts to prefer that level of heat. A flock of Flutter Fires, butterflies that burned like embers, they swarmed their enemies burning any threat to death. When they moved to attack, Tuck isolated the flock from the space around them. Without a fresh supply of oxygen the Flutter Fires suffocated in moments. Adaline was shocked at Tuck's efficient brutality but didn't say anything.

"You don't approve." Tuck said. Adaline's body language was clear as day.

"This is my first time in the wilds, it doesn't seem as bad as everyone says. I feel like we are the invaders here. Those Flutter Flies were just living their lives." She stated.

"Another way to look at it is that we were just passing by when they decided to attack us. You are looking at this from a point of superiority. A superiority that is undeserved. The moment we left The Warren we became just another pair of beasts in the food chain.

Kill or be killed.

Take your readings then we'll rest for the night. From tomorrow we'll be travelling more conventionally." Tuck told her before diving back into his own thoughts. Adaline took the readings while thinking over Tuck's words.

Once Adaline was finished Tuck Wyrmed them to the forest. Out of the direct heat Adaline shivered in the spring like temperatures, her hot sweat turning to frost.

"Just give me a moment and we'll be set." Tuck told her. He found an area clear of massive trees and gestured to a spot. A massive hexagonal pit appeared in the ground then to be filled with an equally massive stone platform.

"Come on." Tuck took Adaline by the hand and led her to the center of the platform. It was convexed, forming a slight hill and at its apex was a circle of runes. Tuck instructed Adaline that she had to put her finger on a particular rune then, without lifting it, slide her finger to other runes in a certain order. Tuck's lock worked like a modern smartphone unlock screen. Tuck walked Adaline through the pattern until she had it memorised and then let her input it into the platform.

The two shimmered and were in a room. It was a prep room much smaller than the platform but with the same Rune structure on the floor. The walls had an enchantment that allowed her to see through them. The view was the same as when they stood on the outdoor platform. Adaline figured it was so you could check your surroundings before exiting. Tuck led her into another room. A work area with a desk, maps and a library of research books.

"Welcome to my Hideaway, let me give you the tour." Tuck showed Adaline the greenhouse, the kitchen and dining room on the next floor. Then down to the recreational area and finally to the bedrooms and baths on the final level.

"Altair this is amazing, I'll admit, I wasn't looking forward to camping in the wilds. Not even the Ward stones I have in my Carry-All bag could offer this type of security." Adaline marvelled.

"Ok, take a shower and freshen up but don't fall asleep, I'll prepare dinner. So come back up to the kitchen when you are ready." Tuck told her before heading back up.

Adaline enjoyed the luxurious accommodations. Until her hunger forced her to seek the kitchen. Tuck had just finished a stew and he served it with fresh bread and fruit juice. Adaline was in heaven. After the meal Adaline was ready for bed but Tuck reminded her of the circlet they had to make.

Begrudgingly she followed him upstairs to the work area. Tuck could have pulled the gold into his Reservoir and shaped it himself but he wanted to see a Mage craft something so he provided Adaline with a block of gold and an energy crystal. Adaline cleared her mind and uttered the spell for levitation and heat. Tuck watched as the gold deformed into a perfect circle with golden wings opened up above the brow creating the perfect setting for a gem. The energy crystal floated above Adaline's other hand as she continued to chant and bit by bit it rotated and was chiselled into a multifaceted marble. The two pieces came together, the marble like energy crystal between the golden wings.

"How is that?" Adaline handed Tuck the finished work.

"Beautiful." Tuck took the circlet and concentrated for a moment before handing it back to her. Adaline saw no change but noticed the little snake eating its tail below the energy crystal. He had engraved it but she didn't notice how. When it came to gold items tuck could skip the injection stage of enchanting.

Putting the circlet on her head Adaline could feel the tingle of enchantment wash over her.

They retired down in the living area. Tuck settled down with a drink to enjoy the night sky. He had enchanted the ceiling on this level to show what was above the Hideaway. The night sky was filled with clouds and shifting mists of different colours. A few moons travelled on their paths but Tuck's strong eyes could see those moons were inhabited, most likely by powerful Sects. There were also floating landmasses that sometimes caught the light.

But there were no stars.

"It's beautiful." Adaline commented as she sat next to Tuck and made herself comfortable.

"I'm a little sad we can't see the suns." He lamented. Adaline laughed.

"There is only one sun Altair." She said. Tuck's mind stuttered, he had meant to say "stars" but in a Dyson sphere like Shaards that only faced inwards no word for "stars" existed.

Tuck opened a Wyrm hole leading outside of Shaards, he adjusted the aperture so dangerous radiation could not get in but allowed a wide range of light so she could appreciate the colours most people would never see. Adaline sat forward, her mouth hanging open. Tuck kept quiet, giving her the time she needed to soak in the splendour. It was a full 10 minutes before she spoke again.

"Altair, what am I seeing, is this the Sacred Realm?"

"Sacred Realm, is that what your people call it? To me it is the infinite void in which the world of Shaards floats.

Each prick of light you see is a sun. Some are younger but many are far older than the sun we see during the day.

The same rationale applies to their sizes, some of those lights are bigger than Shaards itself, they only look like specks because they are so ridiculously far away."

"I'm feeling very small, and truly insignificant." She said with a smirk.

"I'm sorry that was not my intention, I was just trying to share some of the wonders I've seen."

"I thank you for the intention. But you may have damaged my ego. I now have a need to be the center of the world." Adaline climbed into Tuck's lap and kissed him. "Make me the center of your world Altair, for tonight focus on just me."

"I can do that." Tuck held Adaline close and they gently made love under the vision of stars.

***

Adaline awoke to the delicious smell of Derka tree sap, the closest thing to coffee Tuck had found on Shaards.

Still half asleep Adaline rolled out of bed bonelessly. Tuck watched as she meandered a path to him and the breakfast tray he carried. Once she reached him she took one of the cups of warm sap and drank it in one long pull.

A deep sigh preceded her truly opening her eyes. By now Tuck had put the tray onto the table so Adaline pulled him down to her height to give him a quick kiss before heading to the bathroom in a slightly straighter line.

This was Tuck's second time seeing Adaline wake up and he was now sure she wasn't a morning person.

When Adaline came out of the bathroom half an hour later she was all put together. Bouncy and alert like her usual self. Tuck had kept their breakfast in stasis and so the two ate together while planning their route. Adaline used her magic to create a holographic map showing their path thus far.

"We need to keep heading north, all the valleys along this path were super heated. But the other valleys were unaffected. Something is moving underground. With some luck we can continue backtracking it to a point it surfaced in the past. Then I would be able to find out what we are dealing with." Adaline said.

"Ok let's pack up and get a move on." Tuck told Adaline, the two made their way to the top of the Hideaway. Again Tuck had Adaline enter the passcode and they were outside. The early morning air was cool and crisp, there was a light mist over the clearing. Tuck collected his Hideaway leaving a massive hole in the ground.

"Are you not going to refill that?" Adaline asked.

"No," Tuck said. "I'm going to use the soil I collect on this trip to make my own Ecosystem in a part of my Reservoir, so that I can have my own atmosphere. My Titan beast could live in the void but as far as I know I need air, and I have no intention of testing if I can survive without it." Tuck informed Adaline.

"Wow, are you planning on going out there?" Adaline was amazed.

"Not now but I like being prepared. Let's focus on the present." Tuck said, as he scanned the area. He no longer let his concentration lapse while in the wilds. Adaline picked up on Tuck's alertness and also focused on their surroundings. Adaline pressed her back into Tuck, yesterday she got used to him standing behind her to use his teleport.

"You said we are travelling in a more traditional manner today, I have to admit I'm not the most athletic. I have a flying treasure if we need it." Adaline admitted.

"I'll provide transport so you don't need to be athletic and you can save your flying treasure for another time." Tuck said as he activated his shroud. Instead of pulling himself in as usual he pushed his shroud out into local space and spread the dimension like a platform. The Shroud swirled around their feet like a disk of nothingness. Where the 2 dimensions met the atmosphere distorted, creating a storm cloud perimeter. Tuck reigned in his building excitement when he realised he had basically recreated the 'Flying Nimbus' from Dragonball. Adaline sat down, using Tuck's legs as a backrest.

"I don't feel like I'm sitting on a substance. It's both comfortable and weird." Adaline was amazed. She giggled as they briskly rose into the air. This was better than her flying treasure, with Tuck's ability she couldn't feel the acceleration, the wind was blunted to be gentle and the air didn't get colder, not that it would have mattered now that she wore her new circlet. Adaline took in the view for a little bit a few pieces of land floated here and there above the untamed forest below. Satisfied she finally activated her magic and searched the topography for valleys for them to investigate while they flew north at a relatively slow speed.

Tuck concentrated on flying while Adaline navigated. Thanks to her magic, they were able to find the valleys below even when the massive trees hid them from the sky. The trail became clearer but they had yet to find an area where the cause of the heat rose to the surface.

Over the next 3 days the trail got colder. The areas this creature had rested were beginning to recover. The tenaciousness of the forest was reclaiming what was burned.

Just as all hope seemed lost, the couple were amazed to find civilization or at least the remnants of one, this far out. A ruined country built around a volcano. Surrounded by thousands of massive broken Barrier-Pillars shaped like Obelisks. Although the country's glory was in it's past, a smaller city settlement was growing from it's bones. Someone had cobbled 5 working Barrier-Pillars together from the fragments of the broken thousands and a wedge shaped civilization was growing, or maybe dying.

Tuck looked through the spectrum and saw the Barrier-Pillars' magic flicked precariously. They were many times weaker than their predecessors and could fail at any moment.

"Altair that still looks days away but it seems to be in the right direction. Can we get there even if you've never been there before?" Adaline asked.

"Of course we can, we're only travelling at this speed because I don't want to miss a clue." Tuck told her before the world swirled and they were floating above the city gate. Adaline blinked away her confusion and took in the guards and civilians looking up at them. They average around 8 feet tall with skin tones ranging between red and blue. The Demon race.

"Oh shit Altair, we need to run." Adaline said in a panic, she had been told stories about the Demon race her whole life, she didn't want to die. The guard shouted something in it's guttural language. Imagine Adaline's surprise when Tuck laughed and replied in kind.

CHAPTER 12

"Greetings Human, or are you fairy since you are small and floating about." The Guardsman called up to Tuck. Tuck laughed.

"Greetings to you Guardsman, we just came over the forest, what city is this?"

"This is Gorram. Unless you are some bigshot you've got to go to the end of the line if you want to get in." The guard told them.

Tuck took in the crowd of people outside the magical barrier, they lined up hoping to be let inside but the line was moving at a glacial pace and night would soon fall. Despite having a much greater grasp on his abilities Tuck was still not a fan of being exposed at night. He brought them down to the ground and felt Adaline's grip on his arm tighten. She looked back and forth between him and the Guard with a worried expression.

"What's the matter?" Tuck asked her. Adaline blew out a breath of frustration before answering.

"Humans and Demons have been enemies for generations, here you are being friendly to one, how do you even know their language?" she asked exasperated. Tuck kept his poker face in place, he hadn't realised he had switched languages but now he thought about it he could do it at will.

'I really wonder how many languages they squeezed into my noggin.' he thought.

"Look around Adaline, there are a bunch of other species here, a few humans too. This city is more diverse than The Warren but no less peaceful." Tuck said aloud. He had an idea on how to get in. Taking out his Merchant Association plaque, he handed it to the guard who scanned it and nodded. The guard returned the plaque and spoke to another guard inside the barrier.

"It's real, let them in." To Tuck he said. "The Association is the green building down this street. You may also want to get your lady a translation set. Necklace and choker combination. They are expensive but useful for travellers." Tuck nodded his thanks and they entered Gorram.

Adaline was impressed at the reach of the Merchant Association, to have clout even a Demon led community was seriously impressive to her. As they walked Tuck began telling Adaline what he and the guard had discussed.

"Won't an enchanted choker interfere with the magic of my necklace?" Adaline asked.

"Hmm, it should be ok, make sure you wear the choker high up on your neck." Tuck replied while navigating the crowds looking for their destination.

Gorram was packed. There were stalls and makeshift shelters in the streets. With the exception of a few areas kept clear by armed guards Gorram was overcrowded. It was clear the barrier could only contain so many people but no one wanted to sleep outside.

They made it to the association building and Tuck once again used his plaque to gain them access. Along the walk Tuck came across a few enchantments he didn't yet have, he added one that made an item return to a specific place and a complete version of the Barrier-Pillar enchantment.

Once inside they were shown to a comfortable room and treated like VIPs until the branch manager came. He was a blue, one horned demon who wore an orange toga and a plethora of accessories. A circlet, earrings, a choker, a necklace, a bangle on each wrist and a ring on each finger. When Tuck checked his sandaled feet he saw toe rings and anklets as well. Every accessory was enchanted.

"Friend Bashtuck it is rare to get an Enchanter this far out from the comforts of the established cities. Of course that probably has something to do with you being a Bagman as well. My name is Kenon, in my youth I too was a Bagman."

"Greetings Kenon people usually call me Tuck. I've come researching the Calamity that fell Gorram." Tuck rose and greeted Kenon.

"Well you came at the right time, in a few more years not even this outpost will remain." after the greetings Kenon joined them for refreshments.

"You mean because the Makeshift Barrier Pillars are failing?" Tuck said to Kenon, causing the Demon surprise .

"You can see that? You must be very skilled. A country built open like this is a rarity, the Barrier-Pillars kept most monsters at bay but on Shaards, calamity can strike anywhere. Still our Merchant Association is studying these shattered remains hoping to uncover their construction. There is a market for these but I fear it will be decades before we figure it out." Kenon lamented.

"Maybe not, I know how to create these Barrier-Pillars already. Provide the materials and I'll build some, for a price." Tuck told Kenon, this was truly an opportunity for the Association. In The Warren the Clans established the city and thus owned most of it. With enough Barrier-Pillars the Merchant Association could do the same with minimum infrastructure and generate infinite revenue.

"Good brother, name your price. How much do you want for this Enchanter's Manual?" Tuck thought about it and realised no one could match his speed. Business would come back to him so he could afford to let it go to expand his repertoire.

"I'll exchange the Enchanter's Manual for Barrier-Pillars with the Enchanter's Manual for Transit-Gates and of course I want to know about the Calamity that befell Gorram." Tuck told Kenon who in turn weighed his options.

"I can tell you about the calamity now but that Transit-Gate Manual is a highly prized item. I'll need to contact Central, only they would have a copy." Kenon replied.

"In that case Kenon, let me prove my Manual's worth as well as show off my skill so you will fight for me harder. You were once a Bagman, do you have any uncut marble, gold and Energy crystals?" Tuck asked, Kenon concentrated for a moment before taking off one of his rings and giving it to Tuck.

It was a Spatial-ring containing 10 uncut columns of marble, gold to inlay the inscriptions and energy crystals to power it all. Tuck took a moment to study the ring's enchantment, a high capacity Carry-All bag like the one Miriam and Adaline had contained a 10 foot square space, about the size of a garden shed but this Spatial-Ring contained a space about 3000 square feet, that was bigger than a warehouse. Tuck had been stumped at how to pull this off but now he could see the enchantment took advantage of the ring shape to circle back on itself and increase capacity and stability. Overjoyed, Tuck added the enchantment to his knowledge base before he moved 3 of the columns to his Reservoir to effortlessly shape and enchant them into Barrier-Pillars. He placed them back into the Spatial-Ring and returned it to Kenon who looked sceptical at first but soon looked amazed after inspecting the contents of the ring.

"This is… not only can you make them, you can do it so quickly!" Kenon jumped to go make the request to the Association but Tuck stopped him.

"Friend Kenon, there is no need to run off. Sit, tell me about the calamity, you can haggle with Central later while I sleep." Rather than sitting down Kenon made a gesture and a Tome appeared in his hand.

"Here, this is Branch Manager Birkhalt's record of that time. You can read his first hand account for details but the abridged story is a Firecrow descended from the sun wanting to make a nest in the volcano." Kenon called a servant to show them to their room while he went to speak to Central.

CHAPTER 13

The room was opulent but after experiencing the tasteful decor
of Tuck's Hideaway Adaline found the place a bit tacky. She had
remained silent during Tuck's meeting with Kenon because she didn't
understand what was being said so Tuck ordered a translation set
for her since he didn't have time to research and build one himself.
He did, however, add the enchantment for the translation pieces
to his growing list of enchantments and made 3 Signet-rings which
allowed the wearers to make telepathic calls to each other. He further
enchanted two of them to double as Spatial-Rings. He kept the
normal one on his left pinky finger and would give the first Spatial
one to Miriam when he saw her next. If things went well with Adaline
she'd get the next.

After a bath and a meal Tuck and Adaline settled into a comfortable
chair and he began reading the log book of Manager Birkhalt to
her. She took images of the pages and recorded his translations as
evidence.

Birkhalt recorded a solar flare and rising temperatures 3 days before
the calamity hit. A 3 eyed Firecrow descended on the country of
Gorram, their ward pillars withstood one flaming attack after another.
Where humans had Champions and Mages, Demons had Tamers
and Djinn. It was these heroes who rose to face the beast and they
may have been successful if the barrier did not fail. The shockwave
of the explosion hammered the defenders but the Firecrow was
further away and avoided the worst of the blast.

With the defenders down the Firecrow went to the volcano. The
country was built around the volcano because the Demon Djinn used
their magics to syphon the heat to power the country. That same
blessing became a curse as the Firecrow made its nest and laid an
egg.

The defenders rallied and although the destruction was done they
were now focused on revenge. They attacked with abandon, many

had lost loved ones and now all had lost their homes. The Firecrow would know no peace while they breathed.

Before the Firecrow had the advantage of mobility, but it lost that edge trying to protect its egg. It wasn't long before it received enough injuries to make it retreat. Taking its egg The Firecrow dived into the magma but it never surfaced.

Tuck closed the book and exchanged a look with Adaline. She ended the recording and stored it away in her Carry-All bag.

"I bet that bird lost its direction and got trapped in the magma layer of Shaards' outer shell." Tuck said. Adaline blinked at him in confusion.

"You mean the ground, why did you call it a shell?" She asked. Tuck went on to explain that Shaards was a spherical spinning shell built around this sun, and what she believed to be flat earth was the inner wall of the shell. Adaline then wanted to know if the only way in or out of worlds was with a spatial ability like his own. Which led Tuck to explaining how special Shaards was compared to a planet. She was fascinated and peppered him with questions. Tuck answered all he could, encouraging her thirst for knowledge. Hours later the meandering conversation came back around to the Firecrow.

Adaline pulled out her magic mirror and contacted her master Hizanko, telling her an abridged version of what she found out.

"So you are saying it can't break through the metal layer of the earth and is looking for a 'soft' spot. Somewhere magma bubbles to the surface naturally." Hizanko verified. "The Warren is built over a Caldera. Enchantments convert heat into energy. We condense that power into energy crystals we trade with other cities, we use that heat to purity our water and power our city and spells. Now you telling me some shitty 3 eyed reject from the Sun is going to ruin it all! Damn it! Damn it!" Hizanko was distraught. She took a while to compose herself.

"Good work my apprentice. I'll tell the GreatMages of the other Sects and inform our own headquarters. The ArchMage will make the final decision for us. Get a good rest and come home in the morning, we'll need your evidence. I fear the Militia and the Clans will take some convincing. Without The Warren to legitimise their status they are just Mercenaries and Merchants." Hizanko said before bidding her Apprentice good night. She still had no words for Tuck who had the strong suspicion the GreatMage didn't like him very much.

"I still have business to attend to here with Kenon so I won't be able to return with you." Tuck told Adaline. She looked even more downcast than when she was discussing the destruction of her hometown.

"I have this amulet, it will take me directly to my master's side. It's just… I've already become used to waking up next to you." Adaline and Tuck held each other, each lost in their own thoughts. Adaline leaned up and kissed him.

"Let's not waste tonight in melancholy." She said to him with lust in her eyes. Tuck didn't need to be told twice.

***

"Oh goodness that was wonderful." Adaline complimented. "I wish we could be lovers permanently." She lamented. It was now early morning. In a few hours the sun would come out to herald a new morning.

"Sounds great to me, what's stopping us?" Tuck asked.

"Factions. I'm a Halceon Sect Mage and you are an Enchanter in the Merchant Association. My Sect wouldn't even allow us to get married unless you agreed to leave the Merchant Association and become a Bagman for the sect. That is a terrible deal especially since my Sect does not respect anyone who's not a Mage. You would never be an Executive or an Elder, not to mention our reach is nowhere as wide as the Merchant Association." Adaline explained while laying on Tuck's chest.

"Okay, those are the reasons I should not leave the Association but what reasons should you not leave the Halceon Sect?" Tuck asked her.

"Honestly I've learned all I can from my Master. I wear the Rune tapestry of an Expertmage. Being a GreatMage's Apprentice is just a fast track to taking her position in the Sect once she's passed on, in another 20 years I'd be one of the youngest GreatMages in our Sect. Leaving the Sect would cost me power. I'd be set back years! If I left my Sect to join the Merchant Association Mages I would be stripped of my Sect Rune tapestry. I would then have to earn the pieces of the Association's Rune tapestry by performing tasks. Even if you leverage your position in the Association it would still take me another eight years to get to the level where I am currently." Adaline felt a little dejected, despite it not being said in as many words, Mages were slaves to their Sects.

"Other than labouring for every Rune piece is there no way to get a full Tapestry?" Tuck queried. Adaline blew a raspberry.

"Find a full legacy. But that is next to impossible. Entire Sects are built around a single legacy no one will sell one if they had it." Adaline concluded. Tuck pulled a book from his Reservoir.

"Take a look."

Adaline recited a light spell and checked the plain looking notebook. On the first page there was an anatomical black and white drawing with colourful runes on the chest. There were also notes on which type of magical beast the blood used to draw the Runes should be from.

It was the first step in a Rune tapestry.

Adaline sat up.

Page after page the tapestry was filled in. She had never seen a Tapestry like this. To be fair she had only seen the parts of her Tapestry she currently wore but those designs didn't have half the power she was now seeing.

'Could this be the tapestry of an Empire Sect?' She wondered.

"Altair, where did you get this?" She asked with trepidation, if this was some stolen legacy even to have seen it could prove lethal. Tuck's only reply was gentle snoring. Adeline smacked him on the chest with the book, jumping Tuck awake.

"You don't get to drop a bomb like this and go to sleep! Where is this legacy from?"

"I worked it out in my spare time."

"Bullshit, it's already amazing someone your age can be an Enchanter, creating a Rune tapestry would take…" Adaline stopped her tirade short as she looked into Tuck's amused eyes. In the dim light of her magic Tuck's purple eyes seemed to glow with ethereal energy. Tuck could see her mind doing mental gymnastics. The

Goddesses' blessing, his ability to see magic and centuries as an academic had allowed him to reverse engineer the Rune patterns of the 3 Sects and then create his own which had more synergy, could draw more power and granted finer control than the ones he already knew. And it only took him days instead of lifetimes.

"Altair, how old are you?" Adaline asked, her eyes squinting in suspicion. She had come to the wrong but not inaccurate conclusion. Since Tuck had decided to never mention the Goddesses to anyone this would do.

"Would you believe me if I told you 40?" He asked with a grin on his face.

"Of course I would, I'd just ask if that was hundreds or thousands?" She replied. Tuck laughed.

"I must know, are there so many immortals on Shaards? Both you and Miriam have come to that conclusion almost instantly." He queried.

"There is always somebody trying to attain Godhood, the closest any get is some degree of immortality. Of course those types of immortality vary wildly. With some having to go into rejuvenating slumbers while others die and are reborn constantly. Which type are you, I wonder?"

"The type that has no intention of testing his limits."

"Smart, that type never likes what they find. But back to this." Adaline held up the book. "What are your terms?"

"I get you as my second wife, in an Indentureship contract. You get the full Tapestry, straight to Archmage of the Bashtuck Clan. Should you end the contract, you keep the tapestry you wear until you join another Sect at which point the Tapestry dissolves. Should I end the contract the legacy is all yours and you can use it to start your own Sect. In either situation you never speak of where you got the legacy."

"Deal. But I must be allowed to tell my Master why I'm leaving, she has been too good to me over the years."

"That's fine, just tell her my Clan had a full Legacy that I'm offering you. The important information that I don't want spread is that I can create them."

"Understood, once I return to The Warren and give my report I will tell my Master and withdraw from the Sect. Then I can join your Clan."

The two exchanged a passionate kiss, sealing the deal.

By the way Altair, how many wives do you intend to take?

"Hopefully 2 wives should sate my ravenous libido. Of course if you ladies decide you need help feel free to pick a third." Tuck said cheekily, he was expecting some form of retaliation from Adaline but she surprised him with her reply.

"Yeah, that makes sense." Adaline returned the notebook. "Have all the ingredients ready for me when we next meet. I don't want to wait a moment longer than I have to."

"Relax, I already have them. Let me contact Miriam and give her the good news and a head start on the evacuation."

Tuck hadn't bothered to buy himself a 2 way mirror so he opened an aperture to Miriam's apartment, space really was Tuck's bitch.

"Miriam." He called. A few moments later Miriam came out of her bedroom holding her revolver wearing an oversized shirt instead of a nightgown.

"Here I was thinking I misplaced that shirt." Tuck said aloud drawing Miriam's attention to the portal, she looked around and smiled when she saw Tuck and Adaline. Miriam walked up to the Portal with confidence and then leaned through to kiss Tuck passionately.

"Hello husband. I assume Adaline will be joining our Clan?" Miriam asked as she brushed the hair out of the Mage's face with a light touch. Adaline smiled and kissed Miriam the same way Miriam did Tuck.

"Greetings wife, I will be Clan Bashtuck's Archmage." Adaline added.

"Yes she will but we can discuss that later. There are things you need to do as soon as possible. Wake Tisa and Ishram, have them gather their employees and their employees' families discreetly and leave The Warren. The city is in the path of a Calamity." Miriam shivered, The Warren was her home all her life. She had only visited one other city. She didn't want any harm coming to her home even though she had already made up her mind to leave it with Tuck. Tuck continued his instructions.

"Go with Tisa to the Clan banks and close both of your accounts. You can put it in the Merchant Association Bank if you want." Tuck said.

"Altair what about Jalissa's school?" Miriam asked. It was Adaline who replied.

"Chances are the Sects will withdraw from The Warren, disbanding the Academy. Fortunately the Bashtuck Clan is about to gain an Archmage. I'll gladly take Jalissa as my apprentice." Adaline assessment seemed sound to Tuck who changed the subject.

"Good, what is happening with The Warren's Clans, they haven't called me, have they found a work around to transport their wealth?" Tuck asked Miriam.

"They believe they still have time. Their spy network found out you took Adaline on a reconnaissance mission. They will probably approach you with a business contract when you come back." Miriam told him.

"I do know where they are housing those treasures. They have formations to stop people from entering but the room is kept in darkness giving me full access." Miriam had been using her Shadow skills all over The Warren and despite all the artificial light, or maybe because of it, there wasn't a place her shadows couldn't reach. Miriam's experiments with her abilities led her to find out she could use the Shadows as an extension of her senses and her limbs. There were no more secrets from her within The Warren.

Miriam hesitated a moment, Tuck watched the emotions play across her face before she told him what was on her mind.

"My husband, I've become a vigilante." She admitted. Tuck told her to go on and she continued to confess. Although Miriam was no longer a member of the Militia she had no love for violent criminals, many of whom were found dead in dark corners bled out from well placed stabs with her shadow claws. After telling Tuck everything she had done she waited for his admonishment but Tuck nodded.

"In this lawless world killing shitty people is a kindness to society. Even though I'm hesitant to play Judge, Jury and Executioner, I know

evil thrives when good people do nothing. I only have one issue
so far. I don't want any blowback on us. You never know who has
hidden support nor what talent investigators may have. So make
things as random as possible. Use only improvised weapons for your
assassinations, no more shadow claws save those for actual fights.
Go through the nearby garbage for your tools and use your shadows
to manipulate them, never physically touch them, always leave
the weapon behind and if you have the time, scatter the victim's
valuables around them, that will invite the unscrupulous to mess up
the crime scene. Also don't ever keep any souvenirs." Tuck's advice
was shocking and useful. She never expected his support, and had
to resist the urge to climb through the portal and bask in his warmth,
that would lead to other distractions and it was soon time for Jalissa
to wake up. Tuck kissed Miriam again then took out a Signet-ring
similar to his own but sized for her. He slipped it onto her pinky.

"This is a Spatial-Ring, it is leagues better than a Carry-All bag.
Use this to pack up your things." Miriam held the ring with a look of
awe on her face. What amazed her wasn't the Spatial-Ring but the
Ouroboros carving which everyone had come to associate as the
Bashtuck Clan crest, Tuck was gifting her a Clan seal.

Unlike his maker's mark there were words carved backwards in
the ring around the serpent engraving which was also backwards.
Adaline leaned in closer and both women deciphered the words 'TO
BECOME THE DRAGON THE SERPENT FIRST ATE ITSELF!'

"I assume this isn't literal." Said Adaline

"I think it is about self improvement." Miriam said, both women looked
to Tuck for answers.

"It is about self improvement, we are to constantly eat away at our
flaws, refining ourselves into excellence. As for whether or not it is
literal I have no idea. The world of Shaards is bonkers, anything
could happen here." Tuck told them. Both women nodded at that
sentiment. Shaards was unpredictable.

Adaline took out one of her calling cards and gave it to Miriam.

"I'll let you know when I'm back in The Warren. We should keep in
contact." Everyone said their farewells and Tuck closed the portal.

***

Miriam bit her finger and dripped blood onto the ring, Tuck had added a blood lock on the enchantment so she could now feel the space inside and the call function. She would check the call function later, in the space she found some enchanted camping equipment, assorted weapons, potions, ward stones, an Enchanted Map board and a full set of enchanted leathers. All useful things but they left a massive amount of room. Miriam decided she would leave nothing behind since she did not have to.

Miriam merged with the darkness stepping through the shadowy corridors that existed between the pools of light sprinting her way to the Clan's hidden storeroom. This is not what Tuck gave her the Spatial-Ring for but she saw no reason they shouldn't seize this opportunity.

After emptying the storeroom she embeded several treasures in the wall. Tuck's lessons on misdirection came in handy here. She had grown to dislike the Weasel after their last meeting so framing him was perfect.

Wester would find out the Clans were hunting him before they found him and he would run. Making him seem even more guilty.

Mirian returned to her apartment and had a quick shower and got ready for her day. She dressed for battle wearing the enchanted form fitting leathers and the dark jacket and shoulder holster for her new guns.

Not having time to make breakfast, she Shadow-walked to the market to purchase a meal for her friends and family. Until this morning Miriam had thought her Shadow-walk covered a massive distance but since seeing Tuck's portal she realised that 'massive' was relative.

When she touched the Shadows in the room he was in through the portal she realised it would take her a month to cover that distance at full speed and there he was making that hole with no effort at all. After their talk about time manipulation Miriam came to the conclusion that despite telling her to experiment Tuck had barely scratched the surface of what he was capable of. She'd help him stay steady as he figured out more.

With breakfast secured in her Carry-All bag, Miriam wouldn't use the Spatial-ring in public. She returned to her bedroom and woke Jalissa with kisses and tickles, sending her to the bath while she began packing up their apartment using the Ouroboros Signet-Ring to collect everything. Jalissa didn't take long, the two of them then went next door to wake Tisa and her family.

Tisa was now waking up when Miriam came in and laid out an elaborate breakfast on the table. Waking the rest of Tisa's family with the food's delicious smell, Miriam's news was not as pleasant but to their credit Tisa and Ishram believed Miriam immediately. Miriam felt warmth in the centre of her being with the trust Tisa and Ishram showed her.

Tisa stuffed some necessities she needed close at hand into her own Carry-All bag before letting Miriam pack up the rest of the apartment in her ring.

Ishram went out to collect his employees and their family immediately after they worked out a cover story. Which was that Tisa was planning to open a second store in Pitt-City and Ishram was going with her and operating from there from now on. Those who planned to come with him were told to bring their families to look for a new place in the new city.

Ishram's Airship was a magical treasure, so it didn't need a crew to fly it but since his ship could carry Cargo and had 30 cabins for passengers he did employ a Team. His employees consisted of a Co-pilot, 3 Chefs, a Barman, 5 maids, a Manager and 8 Guards who also served as General workers. A total of 20 people including himself.

Tisa's store employed 3 sales girls, 5 labourers and 4 Guards who doubled as general workers. A total of 13 persons if they included her.

Of course some people were unwilling to pack up and move at the drop of the hat but Miriam had impressed on the couple that panic was not good and would risk their family. As such they didn't try to convince anyone. Ishram's Manager couldn't convince her contracted mate to take the trip with a similar story for one of his Chefs. 2 of Tisa's labourers 1 of her sales girls and all of her Guards were not interested in seeing the 'New Store'.

The couple hardened their hearts and made ready to leave that very night.

***

When dawn came Tuck and Adaline had breakfast with Kenon. Afterwards Adaline activated her amulet and returned to her master's side.

With the breakfast over and Adaline gone Kenon got down to business.

"Central office wants to make the exchange, you've got a deal." Kenon was all smiles as he continued. "My commission is no rise in my Association dues for the next decade and 100 Barrier-Pillars from you, paid for by The Merchant Association. To be honest, With how much this will cost, you could probably get yourself another Enchanter Manual."

Once again Tuck needed resources more than money.
"How about this, the Merchant Association will provide material for 200 Barrier-Pillars and I'll give you 100 finished ones and keep the others I make." Kenon noded, that was smart, procuring enough marble gold and Energy crystals would have been pricey.

Tuck thought about his next moves while shaping and Enchanting the Barrier-Pillars.

He needed information on the 'Sacred Realm'. Tuck had already began to grow his own self-contained ecosystem and garden with a water cycle and an artificial sun but that was just for him. But Miriam and Adaline's talk about establishing a Clan along with this situation The Warren faced had Tuck thinking of a more permanent base. But setting down roots WITHIN Shaards was too risky so he planned to set down roots ON Shaards.

The outer shell was deserted, with no sunlight and no atmosphere but Tuck had Barrier-Pillars. He had expertise in building a self contained ecosystem. He could now build Transit Gates leading from his base to anywhere else and he could Wyrm wherever he needed to do his scouting. All Tuck needed now was to choose a secluded spot to build his base.

He figured that in areas where the world's shell was fractured, powerful Sects would have already built their bases. He needed to build his Clan's Sacred Realm in the center of the largest unbroken piece of Shaards.

'On Earth building a ~~CULT~~ I mean a Clan is difficult because people are treacherous but on Shaards contracts made that a simple thing to overcome.' Tuck determined that since contract Law was one of those subjects he had studied during his time trapped in the rift before coming to Shaards, he should put some of that legal double talk to work. His contracts would be iron-clad like Shaards had never seen before.

Finding talented people would take some time but for now Tuck had his Hideaway home which had more than enough room for him and his growing Clan.

Tuck and Kenon completed their transaction. It was late afternoon the same day. Tuck entered his Wyrm hole going towards The Warren. He wondered how far his ladies got with their plans.

CHAPTER 14

Despite how early it was when Adaline returned to The Warren she found her Master already entertaining GreatMages from the other 2 Sects. Adaline had greeted them politely and delivered the recording reliquaries but since then everything has been in turmoil. Trying to get her Master alone became impossible. Every time she tried she was either given a task or told to hold on for a moment that was never going to come. With growing frustration Adaline blocked Master Hizanko's path between workstations.

"Master, there is something I need to tell you in private."

"There is no time now child." Hizanko moved to go around Adaline who maneuvered to continue to impede the GreatMage.

"This is important!" Adaline insisted.

"If it is so urgent just tell me and get it over with." Hizanko replied, her head still buried in some notes as she finally got around the younger woman. Adaline knew what she had to say should be private but Hizanko was being insufferable.

"I'm withdrawing from the Halceon Sect." As Adaline said it the room went quiet. Everyone looked back and forth between the two women. All the colour seemed to drain from Hizanko's face.

The other GreatMages had always been jealous of Hizanko who had such a talented protégé, now the rumours would start about how such a talented up and comer had been mismanaged. The 3 Sects were as close as family but what family doesn't bicker?

Hizanko took a deep breath to compose herself.

"Let's adjourn to my office." She said before walking out with her head held high. Adaline followed her with determined steps. As soon as the two were gone the whispering began.

When Hizanko walked into her office she poured a glass of spirits and gave it to Adaline, gesturing for the younger woman to sit. Hizanko brought the bottle with her when she sat.

"Master I'm sorry." Adaline began but Hizanko stopped her apology.

"No my child, I brought that embarrassment upon myself." Both women were quiet once again.

On their second glass Hizanko spoke again.

"Did I or the Sect leave you wanting, I know I can be difficult."

"No master, the Sect is wonderful and I am very fond of you but an opportunity has arisen." Adaline told Hizanko.

"It's that Bashtuck boy isn't it." Hizanko was exasperated, was Adaline so foolish, to throw away her future for some good wood?

"You've researched him. I've never told you he had a Clan name."

"Of course I researched him, I know he came from some small or long forgotten Clan and I'll admit I did him a disservice when I thought him a lout. That he is an Enchanter shows he has a sharp mind and his Clan obviously had good teachers for him. My guess is he lacked the talent." Hizanko's in depth analysis impressed Adaline.

"Yes, I already found out he enchanted my necklace." Hizanko continued. "But I've impressed upon you how important personal power is. If you plan to buy some broken legacy then even with all your education you'll never compile a spell greater than level 2, like some backwoods conjurer. How much help can that level be in rebuilding a Clan and how long before he notices and moves on?"

"Master if I don't take this opportunity and go with him I will regret it." Adaline began to explain.

"How about I send you out on a 2 year sabbatical, if things are still going well with you two when you come back, we can do the paperwork to make you a full time Journeyman Mage. This way you'll still have the Sect to fall back on and you can be with your young man." Hizanko interrupted Adaline, keeping her protégé was no longer her priority, saving Adaline from herself was.

"Master Hizanko please listen to me fully. What I've been able to piece together is that Altair Bashtuck isn't from a small Clan, but a long forgotten one. One that fell to a calamity. I believe this to be the reason he was so willing to help us investigate. After his Clan fell he wandered the Sacred Realm for a long time." Adaline's admission shocked Hizanko. She emptied her glass in one draw and poured herself another.

"Is he an immortal?" Hizanko whispered. Even a high level Sect wouldn't cross a weak immortal if they could avoid it. Immortals always had time on their side.

"He won't admit it but he doesn't deny it either and he knows so much! He is offering me his Clan's full Empire level legacy, an ArchMage Rune Tapestry." Adaline admitted. She went into the details of the contract which left Hizanko with no comeback. The offer was excellent.

"Master are you still going to try and stop me?" Adaline asked after Hizanko had gone silent looking off into the distance.

"No, you were right. You must seize this opportunity. Let's not put this off, get up, I'll unravel your tapestry and you can go." There was no ceremony, GreatMage Hizanko simply used the authority of her Tapestry and recited a spell to remove Adaline's tapestry. The complex rune work became visible for a moment before flaking off into gentle motes of light.

A few minutes passed before Adaline was officially out of the Halceon Sect. She returned the Sect plaque, her Mage robes and all the equipment she had from the Sect. Now wearing a simple dress and the few Enchanted items Tuck had given her, Adaline recited the entire calling spell. Even though it was a mere few sentences, compared to the gesture it usually took, the difference in speed and power was clear.

"I've delivered the evidence and left my Sect, where should I meet you?" There was no reply to her request but there was a knock on the door.

At Hizanko's gesture the door opened and Miriam walked in.

"Greetings GreatMage Hizanko, I'm Miriam Bashtuck, I'm here to collect Adaline." Miriam greeted them politely. Adaline admired Miriam. When they first met at the restaurant all of Miriam's movements were purposeful, the way she sat, how she watched the other patrons and the way she paid attention without seeming to. It was obvious before that Miriam was a capable warrior but now that purposefulness was enhanced by a predatory grace, Miriam was more than capable now.

Adaline hugged Hizanko goodbye and bounced over to Miriam.

"I'll see you tomorrow at the Council meeting Master Hizanko." Adaline said as the two departed arm in arm. Once outside Hizanko's office Miriam pulled Adaline through the Shadows. They emerged on the upper level of The Warren where the Airships docked. They walked into a Flying treasure shaped like a massive dagger. The ship was aptly named The Flying Dagger and it was the property of Ishram, Tisa's contracted partner. Miriam introduced Adaline to the guards and everyone else she met on their way to the Galley where Jalissa, and her older cousin Cameron were creating an impromptu puppet show for a small crowd of children including Cameron's younger siblings.

A few more families came aboard and Ishram made the rounds to make sure no one else could make it. Once he knew no one else was coming Ishram closed the door and The Flying Dagger departed The Warren. The Dagger accelerated but those aboard noticed nothing. Soon they were cruising, at this speed it would take a week to reach Pitt City. They would be able to set up this small group of people before word got out that something was wrong at The Warren and prices at the other Cities skyrocketed.

Once The Flying Dagger was on its way Ishram called all the adults to a meeting room. With Tisa by this side holding his had he told the gathered group about the Calamity heading to The Warren. There were immediate complaints by people who left others behind. Others wanted to know details of what was coming and to see evidence of the Calamity.

"This wasting of time is why none of you were told." Miriam stood up and spoke to the crowd. "Had I not joined a Clan none of us would know death was upon us until it was too late. Be grateful Ishram and Tisa gave you this chance, and those of you who still hold a grudge can go their own way in Pitt city," MIriam was pissed at the people who turned into a panicked mob. She grabbed Adaline by the hand and led them out of the meeting room and to their Suite. Ishram had insisted She and her Clan took one of the better cabins, It had 3 bedrooms and a common room. Miriam slumped on the couch, her mind preoccupied, could she do more? Adaline kneeled down in front of Miriam and took her hands.

"You are beating yourself up over something beyond you. Saving a few is better than saving none and saving all would have been impossible." Adaline told her. The two shared an intimate silent moment holding each other.

"My timing is perfect." Tuck said as he appeared in the room. Both women kissed him and he held them for a moment before getting to business. He handed Adaline the Indentureship contract to sign. She read through it with haste and signed below Tuck's signature. Tuck took out a second Signet / Spatial-Ring sized for her and slipped it on Adaline's finger.

"Welcome to the Bastuck Clan." Kisses were exchanged. "Ok, now strip." Tuck said. Miriam and Adaline dragged Tuck into the master suite. Adaline chucked her simple dress and Miriam locked the door. When Miriam went to take off her leathers and Adaline tried to undress Tuck he stopped both of them, laughing at the misunderstanding. "We have time for sex later, I'm applying Adaline's Tapestry, I don't like her being so weak." Both women looked embarrassed, Miriam opened the door but stood next to it acting as a guard.

"I'll make sure you two aren't disturbed." MIriam said.

It took hours to apply Adaline's Rune tapestry, Tuck had already collected the necessary beast blood and herbs to paint the runes. It took precise control to put down an even layer perfectly. In a Sect a GreatMage would be needed to apply any part of a tapestry but with Tuck's control of space he was more than capable. By pushing his space into the local one, he was able to move objects about with great precision. It was only in hindsight that Tuck realised that this was how his Spatial Awareness also worked.

Adaline was calm and focused on being still, as Tuck floated her and painted her from the soles of her feet to the tip of her head. Tuck's training granted him fine control that even allowed him to paint runes around the follicles of hair on her head. After every completed level Tuck would pause, there would be a deep gong heard and the runes would disappear and would only reappear when Tuck started building another level. Through the gong Miriam was able to estimate what level Adaline had reached. NoviceMage, InterimMage, AdeptMage, ProfessionalMage, ExpertMage, MasterMage, GrandMage,

GreatMage, DivineMage and ArchMage.

The tapestry turned invisible, Adaline continued to float, now under her own power as she explored the limitations of her new ability. Tuck got up and stretched, despite being so busy, he had moved even less than Adaline had.

Miriam had not been idle while those 2 were busy, she had taken in Jalissa and her cousins so Tisa and Ishram could be alone. Miriam saw the kids fed and had the girls sleeping in one room and the boys in the next. She also got dinner brought for the adults and was keeping it warm in her Signet-ring. Tuck used this time to study the Flying Dagger. His Hideaway was already a low level magic treasure, on the dagger he saw some movement enchantments he may be able to modify. Adaline came out of her trance and all 3 adults ate a meal together before piling into bed and falling to sleep.

***

Adaline wasn't a morning person by any stretch of the word. Most mornings it took at least a shower to wake her up but this morning she awoke to Miriam's breathless moans and Tuck's thrusts shaking the bed. Adaline turned to see her two lovers watching her. Their eyes glowed one Purple the other Red both burned with lust. Adaline was now wide awake. She rinsed her mouth with some water by the bedside before crawling over to her spouses. Miriam greeted her with a passionate kiss and an invitation to sit on her face. Adaline did as she was asked, once again she noticed both her lovers were hard of muscle, even Miriam's curves were solid muscle under pliable flesh. Miriam reached another climax, she had stopped counting by now, after the blank moment of euphoria she found herself face to face with her short wife. Miriam met Tuck's eyes over Adaline's shoulder as the slapping noises of him trusting into Adaline filled the room. Miriam kissed her deeply, she found the younger woman irresistible. She was beautiful, her large breasts and soft body were too erotic. Miriam fondled, squeezed, pinched and caressed everywhere. It didn't take long for Adaline to climax. Tuck whispered in both ladies ears the things he loved about them all the while changing positions. At one point Adaline held Miriam's leg over her shoulder while they rubbed their sex together, Tuck was drinking water and catching his breath for another round when he tilted his head as if he noticed something.

"Sorry ladies, we're going to have to cut this session short." He hopped back into the bed and pinned both women face down, a hand on each's back. Using his shroud Tuck formed 4 phalluses and inserted them into his wives before vibrating them rapidly. Adaline lowered her head, raised her hips and gripped the sheets tightly. Miriam tried to push herself up but could only thrash about since Tuck held her down with little effort. Both women became lost in bliss.

His work done, Tuck hopped out of bed and cleaned himself off using his Maw. He then got dressed in a light short sleeve shirt and short pants before leaving the room. Through the door Miriam heard him speaking.

"Good morning kids. Miriam and Adaline are resting, let me make you breakfast. I'm making Pancakes… WHAT? You don't know what Pancakes are …"

"What a beast." Miriam whispered.

"More." Adaline groaned. Miriam laughed and pulled Adaline into a hug.

"Let's just grab a shower instead." Weak kneed, both women wobbled to the bathroom for girl talk and a wash.

The ladies joined the rest late for breakfast. Miriam took the boys to bathe and Adaline dragged the girls to the other shower while Tuck cleaned the breakfast wares.

Today was the day of the council meeting, Thanks to Tuck and Adaline, instead of a meeting to start an expedition it was now a meeting to determine if to evacuate. The advanced time table may save lives.

Jalissa was staying aboard the Flying Dagger with her aunt and cousins, the rest of Clan Bashtuck were headed back to The Warren. Tuck and Adaline were going to testify and Miriam to see if she could do anything for her friends and neighbours now that her family was safe.

Both Miriam and Adaline insisted on a unified look for this official meeting so Adaline used her magic to darken Tuck's and Miriam's leather armors to black. The magic robes Tuck had bought for her at Gorram were already black. They all wore environmental necklaces, shield belts and the most comfortable boots ever. Stacked with the Enchantments on the leathers and robe they were each a walking tank. Their ensemble was finished off with teal coloured Boat Cloaks with orange trim emblazoned with black Ouroboros on the back. They meant to leave a mark.

Tuck held his women and Wyrmed to The Warren. The auditorium where the Council met was already filling up. Rumours had begun to spread about problems with The Warren's cooling system, so people came to find out the truth.

The Bashtuck Clan were escorted to their seats by an AdeptMage, since the Mage's Assembly had called the meeting it was their duty to host. Most VIP guests were escorted by a NoviceMage but Adaline did not hide her overwhelming Aura. Knowing an Archmage was among them put the Mage's Assembly on their best behaviour.

It wasn't long before the 18 council members arrived, 3 from each faction plus 3 members chosen by the people.

GreatMage Hizanko informed everyone that The Warren faced a Cataclysm. An uproar went up immediately, Hizanko waited for quiet before continuing her presentation. People were people and despite the evidence, the testimony and the threat to lives there were many deniers. The Militia believed they could defeat this beast, although all evidence pointed to it surfacing from under The Warren. By the time there would be a fight everyone in The Warren would be dead. The Clans put out appeals about protecting your home while the Merchant Association and Mage Assembly advocated evacuation but the appeals from Militia and Clans were swaying public opinion. The meeting ended with no consensus.

Tuck watched chaos roll across the Council room. As he got up the Bashtuck Clan was approached by several Council members. The first to speak to him was the local Clan head Ms Danub.

"Greetings Headman Bashtuck, had I known your lineage when we first met I would not have been so reluctant to take up your offer." She said.

"That doesn't mean we can't do business now, but since the cat is out of the bag my price goes up to a 5th." Tuck replied with a smile. Headwoman Danub's face turned sour.

"Sad to admit, we've been burgled. The Weasel, Mr Wester found our largest vault and made off with everything in it. So the opportunity is lost." It was Tuck's turn to look sour. Since Miriam had already told Tuck about her heist he acted shocked and angry at his potential loss. Ms Danub continued.

"It is fortunate that our legal holdings dwarf our hidden ones but we can move those with manpower." As Headwoman Danub concluded speaking, Director Opcide joined the conversation.

"Since your business deal fell through you can get your Spatial-Ring by tonight to help speed things along." Opcide's statement made a couple of Clan heads upset.

"If we had that already we wouldn't have been robbed!" Headman Loreth shouted.

"That's my fault Headman Loreth," Tuck admitted. "I'm a master Enchanter for the Merchant Association. Enchanting Danub's Signet-ring was bad for my business." All Loreth could do was fume, Headwoman Danub sighed.

"The ring would be helpful going forward. Please have it delivered as soon as it is ready." Danub said to Opcide before giving a departing bow. She and the other Warren Clans left, as one of the groups advocating remaining they had a lot of organising to do.

"They are going to get a lot of people killed." Said Opcide. Tuck agreed with her, the thing to do was cut losses and run. At this point The Mage Assembly led by GreatMage Hizanko joined the impromptu gathering. Hizanko began tearing up as she hugged Adaline. She could feel the power of an ArchMage coming off her former apprentice and was overjoyed the child had not been misled.

"Congratulations on your Contrat." Hizanko forced the words out through her tears, by this time Adaline was in tears too. Hizanko turned and hugged Tuck, which took him by surprise.

"I don't care how powerful you are, if you break her heart, I'll break your face!" Hizanko sobbed into Tuck's chest. Their exchange brought a round of chuckles. While the GreatMages paid their respects to ArchMage Adaline, Hizanko composed herself to speak again.

"It is unfortunate that there is no time to celebrate. The Sects are sending Bagmen to pack up our Warren Base. A skeleton crew will remain nearby on an Airship Magic Treasure to monitor the situation."

"Let's have lunch in a few days, GreatMage Hizanko, there is something I I'd like to talk to you about." Tuck offered. Hizanko nodded, obviously curious about what he wanted to discuss. Of course Tuck gave no clue.

As the Mages left the Merchant Association delegation permanently attached itself to the Bashtuck Clan, Director Opcide recognised a rising power when she saw it.

'Best to get in on the ground floor.' She thought as she watched The Militia group walk over to speak to Tuck. Major Iskandar, known amongst the troops as Momma, made the introductions.

She presented General Pike to Headman Bashtuck. General Pike was a massive man, 6 foot 5 inches of solid muscle with a neat, disconnected undercut hairstyle and a Garibaldi beard, all his hair was stark white and his eyes were stormy grey. Tuck couldn't tell if his hair colour was an indication of his age or just another in the myriad of colours he had already seen, thus far older folks' hair were just duller.

"Well met Headman Bashtuck." Pike said as he and Tuck shook hands. Pike's attention was drawn to Miriam.

"Congratulations Miriam, glad to see you bounce back. The incident with Lixor was unfortunate but I still believe his assessment to be correct; we needed Champions in the field, not behind a desk." Miriam didn't back down, looking Pike in the eye and replying.

"Then you should include that in your Marketing campaigns. I put in the time and effort, I was even given accolades for going above and beyond my duties. Yet I was passed over for promotion to Captain 3 times because I wanted a desk job. What is really upsetting is that Commander Lixor, who was adamant against me, is a CHAMPION with a DESK JOB!" Miriam's rebuttal left the General embarrassed. Major Iskandar came to his rescue.

"The Militia broke their word to you, which is a shame but fate put you where you needed to be to have the last laugh." Tuck thought Iskandar's words were a bunch of gobble-the-goop, especially since he knew his being here was the result of a FUBAR by 4 Goddesses but Miriam held his hand tighter, obviously mollified. General Pike turned his attention back to Tuck.

"I was wondering what the Bashtuck Clan's position was on this incident?"

"We are definitely leaving." There was no hesitation nor weighing the pros and cons.

"The Warren is done for General, it's time to save lives." Tuck said before excusing himself. He and his ladies departed the council chamber accompanied by Director Opcide. Adaline cast a spell and the din around them dimmed.

"Is the Merchant Association going to evacuate?" Tuck asked Opcide.

"Of course, there is no profit in being trampled. There is a standard but hefty price paid to Bagmen willing to participate in Emergency moves, can I count on you?"

"Sure. There is also a business opportunity here. The Merchant Association has massive Transit-Gates in the Capital cities. I happen to know the enchantments necessary for building Transit-Gates. We can build one just outside The Warren."

"I see," Opcide said, she thought about the possibility for a few moments before continuing. "We can set up 5 tiers. Super wealthy, well off, middle class, poor and destitute. The Super wealthy can be sent to a Capital city, while the well-off can be sent to a lesser city and so on. The destitute we take as slaves to the association and sell them off wherever we can." Tuck flinched when she said this as if he was physically hit. Tuck wasn't above using a Slave contract, despite how Director Opcide had explained it. He knew the Clan contracts she had shown him were also slavery but in those contracts people sold themselves into slavery through greed. In this situation giving desperate people no choice was a true evil.

"Director Opcide we will offer Indentureship Contracts, we'll set a wage rate so they can labour and pay off their debt." Opcide gave Tuck a curious glance.

"You dislike slavery, Headman Bashtuck." It wasn't a question, but one was implied.

"I don't believe debt is a good enough reason to take away a sentient creature's future permanently." Tuck responded.

"Fine," Opcide said, dropping the subject. "We'll do things your way, the real issue is the poor tier. No one is going to want low class labourers with little skill and less prospects added to their city."

"You may wish to contact Kenon of Gorram city. They are about to go through a massive expansion, they need citizens." Tuck told Opcide about Gorram and offered his labour in creating the Transit-Gates for the 2 locations. Once back in her office she and Kenon were able to talk over the Merchant Association's Contact Mirrors. Getting a Mass Transit-Gate for his city at the cost of the materials and gaining residents was too good of an offer, even if Tuck insisted on getting double the amount of materials a mid-sized Gate would need.

Now all they needed was time.

CHAPTER 15

Tuck sent Miriam to spread the word amongst the population and the Militia about the Mass Transit-Gate the Merchant Association was putting up. Knowing there was a plan in place would stop the spiral into hopelessness. Adaline accompanied Miriam while Tuck and Opcide went to the warehouses. Like the 3 Sects the Merchant Association had their own floor in The Warren, the majority of which was storage. Magical wonders like Carry-All bags and Spatial-Rings didn't stop time nor could they hold living things the way Tuck's Reservoir did, if someone didn't want their produce to rot or their energy crystals to deplete, then bulky special stasis containers were needed. As far as the eye could see containers and chests of all sizes were stacked to the ceiling. Tuck waved his hand and the room emptied, leaving Opcide wide eyed.

"I don't think I've ever seen a Bagman with either your capacity or your range. We'll be able to make this move easily." She marveled.

Tuck was about to reply with a witty retort when The Warren shook. One of Opcide's Mates caught her mid fall and Tuck was instantly in his Wyrm hole, although he remained visible. He and Opcide exchanged a worried look before bedlam ensued.

Tuck activated his Time Stop but the devastation was happening so instantaneously he could see it creeping. At most a handful of people, the most powerful, would survive this incident, Tuck had no intention of being a hero but found himself one of the few who could act.

In the past Tuck couldn't interact with the world while in his Wyrm hole but he trained himself to refine his skill, so he could disentangle the myriad of abilities the Wyrm hole brought. Now he could be invisible in his Wyrm hole without activating the Time Stop, an ability he used to spy on the Warren Clans. He could be in his Wyrm hole intangible without being invisible, making himself seem like a ghost. Most important at this point Tuck could be in his Wyrm hole with his Time stop active and use his Maw and Reservoir to affect the world.

His Spatial Awareness pulsed out covering The Warren, Tuck took in the situation, he wasn't the only one able to react to this instantaneous disaster.

A couple of Archmages within The Warren moved quickly, including Adaline who was in the Mage Association. She had cast a spell called 'SAFEHOLD', it erected a powerful force field and pulled people into it. The spell was supposed to be instantaneous but in his accelerated state Tuck saw it travel as a shockwave, those touched by blast vanished, reappearing within the barrier. The rescue was outpacing the destruction so this floor would be secure, Tuck would be able to pull Adaline and those under her protection into his Reservoir at the last moment so he focussed his attention elsewhere.

Using their connection, Tuck searched for Miriam. His sense led him to a section of the residential area occupied by a tyrannical darkness. He could see people caught mid scream as they were devoured not realising that the Shadow was their salvation. Miriam was beyond him, but she would be safe. Tuck would be able to link up with her after the disaster.

As Tuck's sense went wider into the Warren whenever it touched a person he pulled them into his Reservoir but even as he gathered more and more people, the devastation was getting worse. He was stretching the moment as far as he could but was nearing his limits.

He snatched the Airships on the upper levels as well as the food reserves and livestock on the Agricultural level. He hoped the other Bagmen in The Warren would have other supplies since he had no time to search.

Major Iskandar was doing the same with the Militia, gathering them up with her hollow space, she was a Champion with a Mountain Tortoise Soulbeast, she would be tough but not fast. She may be able to survive the blast but could not escape it so Tuck marked her to snatch up on his way out.

Here and there he came across a few champions, most likely with some form of energy based Soul beast, who mastered their abilities to the extent that they were rushing about trying to save people and escape. It was a tragedy their power protected them but not those they tried to save. The would-be heroes wrapped people in thick blankets soaked in the fountain before trying to move them but friction caused problems. Still, burns could be healed, death was the end.

Tuck took mercy on the heroes and the rescued by pulling both groups into his reservoir. Those Champions who could move were put into a separate space from the general population, to protect the normal folks from any shenanigans. Few other places he came across Mages with enough battle experience to have activated their incredibly powerful force fields, Tuck snatched them up too, force fields and all.

By now the pyroclastic material extended from the power plant below the Warren to the docks above, it was time to go.

Tuck Wyrmed his way out of the Warren, for the first time he headed South. Beyond the mountain range The Warren occupied was a narrow valley that opened to a grassland with a lake, surrounded by more forest and a road that ran from The Warren to other City states. Tuck chose to put down 16 Barrier-pillars to form a 9 by 9 grid covering 10 miles. He swept the area with his Spatial Awareness and removed all the magical beasts lurking about. He then placed Barrier portals between sections to act as doors before he exported all the people he had gathered, the animals he dropped into one segment by themselves. People looked around dazed and amazed. A loud explosion pulled their attention up the mountainside to the Warren exploding.

The screech from the massive burning bird rising out of the eruption sent a shockwave rolling over the land.

The blast wave would have killed them if not for the Barrier-pillars. The massive 3 eyed crow spread its wings and took to the sky, turning into beam of light heading towards the sun, it was followed by a flock of 8, the eggs it had come to lay all those years ago had grown up, the Shaards magma layer acting as a substitute for their natural environment the Sun. Now the smaller birds took to the sky for the first time, accelerating until they were also beams of light heading to the sun.

Then they were gone and so was The Warren.

Tuck sat on his shroud, floating above the crowd with Opcide and her entourage standing behind him. People were in tears as the realisation that their home was gone dawned on them. While the survivors went through the stages of loss the powerful leaders sought Tuck out. The Barrier-pillars and portals were all marked with the

Bashtuck symbol and Tuck floating on his cloud made him easy to find.

The Mages who had managed to raise their shields made their way over to Tuck. They could sense the same power that moved them emanating from him. Hizanko led them.

"Senior, thank you." She said as she bowed her head. Tuck made an upset face.

"That is too polite a greeting, you are my second wife's elder." Tuck replied

"I was thanking you on behalf of our Sects, but I am sorry for the way I treated you before Altair, I was hoping we could start anew at that upcoming dinner but let's start now. Thank you Altair for saving me." Hizanko smiled.

"You are welcome Hizanko." Tuck replied, Hizanko looked about a bit before asking.

"Where is Adaline?" She asked.

Tuck pointed to a clearing where his 2nd wife spoke with 2 other Mages.

"She conviens with others of her level." He pointed out to Hizanko. As the lesser Mages went to greet the greater ones Tuck concentrated on his connection to his wives to find Miriam. She and a troupe of refugees were getting closer but had not emerged from the Shadow realm. He sent Miriam a message through their Signet-rings. She and the crowd emerged from a shadowy overhang high up the mountainside. A portal opened and they were Wyrmned to the refugee area.

"There you are." Tuck said. He got up and hugged her, Adaline hurried over to share the embrace. They had survived and were back together.

CHAPTER 16

The survivors of The Warren grieved for a few days. During this time Tuck and Opcide jumped to Gorman to contact the Merchant Association headquarters and let them know what happened. Tuck built a midsized Transit-Gate in Gorman, and collected the materials to build another Transit-Gate. Once Opcide received a replacement Management level Communication mirror they returned to the refugee camp.

Tuck let it be known that in 3 months he would be retracting his Barrier-Pillars and leaving. There were loud protests but no one was in a position to stop him. Opcide announced that the Transit-Gate was operational and let everyone know those who couldn't pay needed to sign Indentureship contracts. More impotent protests followed. In the end The Sects paid to use the Gate to recover their personnel, the Warren Clans joined the Merchant Association and paid for passage to a moderate City state where they would rebuild their fortunes. The Society of Crafts and Engineering wasn't as wide ranging as the Merchant Association but they could still rely on their members in other branches to take them in. The common people signed the contract with the Association, selling themselves into servitude. In the end the only group with no recourse was the former members of the Militia. What city would welcome an army with unknown allegiance? Many members of the Militia took Association's indentureship contract.

By the end of the 2nd month the refugees were relocated to different cities and the Militia was down to half strength. Tuck rented 4 Pillars to Major Iskandar. As a Bagman, she could make use of the massive Obelisks.

The Bashtuck's left and met up with Captain Ishram and Tisa in Pitt City. Tuck contacted a few people he liked for a social get together.

***

The dinner Tuck organised was supposed to be an intimate affair but it ballooned into a massive event. He invited Opcide and her Husbands, Hizanko who brought the 2 GreatMages from the other Sects, General Pike and Major Iskandar from the dwindling Militia. There were also senior members of the Society of Crafts and Engineering.

With the exception of the caterers, the band and Tuck's wives there wasn't a soul there under the age of 60. Despite this the party was upbeat with people looking forward to what they would do next rather than mope about what was lost.

After the meal, Tuck stood and gathered everyone's attention.

"I'd like to thank you all for coming out and celebrating the beginning of the new Bashtuck Clan. Right now the Clan is just me, my 2 wives and my adopted daughter. But Clans, like plants, need deep roots and adaptability." Tuck turned to Hizanko who was sitting next to Adaline.

"Hizanko, my understanding is that you are not from a Clan, but to my wife Adaline you are her only relative an Aunt in all but blood. I extend to you an invitation to Clan Bashtuck." Tuck reached out a hand to Hizanko who hesitated.

"I have invested too many years into the Halceon Sect to leave now."

"I don't want you to leave your Sect, I just spoke about adaptability that includes diversity, we don't all have to be together to be a Clan. being in a Clan just means you have some place to fall back to, so you prioritise the Clans interests above all others. I am sure that they are already members of the Halcyon set that belong to Clans, you will be no different than them." Tuck told her, Hizanko's hesitation evaporated. She reached out and took Tuck's hand. Hizanko felt a moment of fleeting dizziness, the room had gone silent. She looked around and everything seemed to be clearer but everyone stared at her wide-eyed and astonished.

"What?" She asked. Adaline was first to respond.

"From now on I'm calling you big sister." Hizanko accepted Adaline's hug but was still confused. GreatMage Rodert exclaimed.

"Hizanko you've regained your youth!" She looked around surprised, finding her way to the hallway mirror. She reminded herself she was in public to stop herself from stripping. Finally she turned to Tuck.

"How?" She managed.

"It's part of my power set. Physically you are 21 again. I plan to treat my Clan more like a Sect. Contributions will gain Clan members time which they can use on whomever they wish. I haven't worked out all the details but once a year I'll host a 10 day gathering where crowds can shed years. The minimum being a decade."

"Let's call them Contribution Tucks." Adaline chirped.

"But I'm called Tuck, that's going to be confusing." Tuck complained.

"You need to stop introducing yourself as such." Miriam said. "You are no longer the last Tuck, every member of the Clan will be a Bashtuck. From now on you are Altair, Headman of the Bastuck Clan, and you are not alone." Miriam's words touched Altair deeply, he lovingly took her hand and kissed it before Major Iskandar interrupted.

"Pardon Headman Altair, are you recruiting?"

"Yes, rather than only investing in the young and then waiting for them to mature, I am also offering those of great power something they can't get on their own. Their youth. Of course Hizanko was a special case, everyone else will need to sign the Clan Contract first."

The floodgates were opened, even the caterers wanted to be Clan servants. They met everyday to iron out the responsibilities of the Clan elders, what was considered a contribution, what the Clan could provide and the costs they would charge versus the costs of things outside the Clan.

Of course talks about the location of the main Clan came up, Altair informed them of his breaking ground in an area of the sacred realm. The crowd was sufficiently awed, the Bashtuck Clan would grow from strength to strength, built around Altair as the lynch pin.

END

AFTERWORD

Yay, you made it!

I love stories set in another world.

For me it started with Enid Blyton stories like the Faraway tree and the wishing chair. Then I came across space adventures like Buck Rogers which did the same thing, replacing magic with a spaceship but it was still a new world to explore before returning to safety of your blankets and pillows.

As I grew older I moved up to age appropriate literature. I found less of those wonderful tales of escape and more tales of hopelessness where we rolled from one malicious circumstance to another. If it was a one shot you would be lucky if the protagonist survived and if it was a series the hero never seemed to improve their lot from book to book. The protagonists just couldn't seem to catch a break and we, the readers, were forced to choke on their misery.

It wasn't for me.

I did enjoy the addition of sex in the books but not the drudgery that seems to follows adults through the work week.

If you can't find what you are looking for, make it yourself.

This book is my attempt to have a more light hearted adventure. There are parts where adversity must be overcome but the tone isn't bleak.

I really hope you enjoyed the read and please leave a review. My understanding is that it helps the book get seen.